MASTER SHANGO
PRESENTS...

Damien Dsoul

Master Shango Presents...
First published in 2013
This edition published in 2017 by
House of Erotica
www.houseoferoticabooks.com
an imprint of
Andrews UK Limited
www.andrewsuk.com

Contents

MASTER SHANGO PRESENTS...

Pimp Zee: The Life Of…

Zee drove to his pad after two hours of playing basketball at one of his friend's courtyard. His apartment was situated in a condo suit overlooking the crystalline waters of Frisco Beach. The neighbourhood was quiet and ultra-modern, and though the price tag had been kind of a cut-throat to settle, he felt good having secured it, knowing a lot of brothers out there would be just as envious to be holed up in an area like this.

He entered his lush apartment, dropped his gym bag and face towel on a couch, threw his car keys on a coffee table and went into the bedroom. He showered then went into the kitchen to make himself a sandwich. He put on a jazz album in his disc player then went into the kitchen to drink some water. Having cooled off a bit, he returned to his bedroom to sit at his desktop computer to check his online emails and correspondences. He smiled when he saw that he'd caught another woman's attention with the thread post he'd made a couple of days ago at an interracial online forum site dedicated towards interracial dating and hook-ups. In the discussion thread he'd asked the question if there were any white women out there desiring a chance of wanting to be pimped. Pimping was his game, and if any sexy women around felt the need for a taste of black experience and more, then they need not look any further. He'd left his email address at the end of the thread and wrote that they should give him a shout-out whenever they feel like it. Two women had already contacted him, and now here was a third. He clicked on the mail and began to read:

Hi there Pimp Zee,

My name's Marilyn. I read your thread at the __ forum and would like to get in touch with you regarding it. I've got a '36DD pair of tits, and I've got a thick ass to match LOL. Please write to me or even better call me at this number below. Can't wait to hear from you.

Bye.

Zee scribbled down her phone number on a pad then checked through his other mails before deciding to give her a call. The phone rang a third time before being picked up. The woman at the other end of the line said "Hello" into his ear. She had a nice sounding voice; Zee hopped that it was Marilyn and not someone else.

"Hi, my name's Pimp Zee, and I'm calling—"

"Oh my God," the woman exclaimed delight in her voice. "Hi there, Zee. This is Marilyn on the line."

"Hi Marilyn. I just finished reading your mail that you sent me and thought I'd give you a call."

"Thanks for calling, Zee. Tell me, is that really your name or something you picked up?"

Zee couldn't help but laugh; it had been a long time since anyone thought it curious to inquire about his nickname. "My real name is Zeke Darren, but people know me as Pimp Zee. Pimping is what I do, which is pimp lovely white chicks."

"White chicks who love tasting black meat, is that it?" she chuckled into his ear.

"Yep that's it, babe. So how about you telling me a little about yourself?"

"Well, Marilyn is my first name. I'm in my mid-thirties, being married for thirteen years with three kids; I work part-time at an animal shelter and I enjoy knitting."

"That sounds nice. In other words, you're a homely type of woman."

"Well, if you want to put it that way, yeah I am. I hope that's not disappointing?"

"No, it really isn't. I do enjoy hooking up with homely women. So now tell me about your love life. You enjoy having sex?"

"Oh yes, I love having it. Just that my darling husband can't keep up with me at all, so I've had to look outside for assistance."

"All right, that's good to hear. So tell me why you're interested in wanting to get pimped?"

Girlish laughter echoed in his ear before Marilyn answered. "Well it's like this. As I said already, my husband has for a long time been unable to satisfy me in bed, and it's been quite frustrating for me. He enjoys knowing that there're men out there clamouring for me, and several times I've gone out of me to get other men's attention. They've all been white, and though the few ones I've been with have been somewhat good … I still feel incompletely satisfied about it. Since I became a member at that forum, seeing naked pictures of some of the black men in there … and also picking interest in watching interracial porn movies (another pause for giggle) anyway, I just feel that I need to try me some big black cock. I can't help picturing myself getting used like the white girls in those adult movies. And when I saw your thread post … well, you get the idea don't you?"

"Yes, I sure do." Zee was growing a noticeable erection just from listening to her chatter. He pulled down his zipper and unearthed his tool out of his shorts and began stroking it while at the same time nodding his head to her words. "So tell me Marilyn, ever deep-throated anyone before?"

"Err … well … I really wouldn't know …"

"Alright let's side-step that for now. How about anal sex, ever tried it?"

"No, no, I haven't … not really looking forward to it yet … maybe in the future when I'm like ready enough. It scares me."

"It's always scary at first, but trust me later you'll come to love it.

Two other questions for you: where are you right now and what're you putting on?"

Another round of girlish chuckle—Zee couldn't help it—he was really liking this woman. Just the sweet sultriness in her voice was getting him hard right there. He reckoned she would go far by the time he was done breaking into her.

"I've just returned home from work and I'm in my kitchen right now fixing dinner, and I'm putting on a tank top and a brown skirt. Why did you ask?"

"Just trying to take note is all. Are you feeling randy right now?"

A pause. "Well ... I don't know if I should—"

"Well you should know, Marilyn," Zee went on stroking his cock, his voice sounded serene as if he was talking in his sleep. "Let's say a black man was in there standing right next to you right now and he really wanted to fuck you, tell me what would you say to him? Let your imagination run wild on this one."

"I don't know, I've never been surprised that way before ... but since you asked, I guess I'd forget about cooking dinner and let him have me."

"That's not the appropriate sentence to use, Marilyn. Tell me you'd let him fuck you. Say that for me."

"Okay, I would love for him to fuck me. How does that sound?"

"Perfect. When was the last time some guy made you cum? And I'm talking about explosive cum. The kind that rattles your inside all the way to your bones."

She thought for a moment, then said: "I'm not going to lie to you, it's been so long—maybe while I fucked one of those white guys a month ago. I can barely remember it."

"Hmmm, too bad. I'll bet you're anxious to want to experience that again?"

She didn't hesitate with her answer. "Oh yes, yes, yes ... very much, I'd love to."

"Has your husband ever been there watching you getting fucked before?"

"Once, though the last time I did it was in a motel, though I did tell him about it afterwards. I know he wouldn't mind seeing me getting fucked by a black man. I think he'd go crazy just to see me getting used."

"What about your kids?"

"They're away in college. The house is only me and Danny my husband."

"That's good to know. So you'd really like for me to give you the black cock hook-up, right? Better say it loud so I know you mean it."

"Yes!" she affirmed. "Yes, I'd love nothing more than to have my first taste of black cock. I've seen, read and heard so much about it, I'd really love to try it for myself."

"Very well then." His hand left stroking his erection and reached for his pen and jotter pad. "I'm going to swing by your house and get a taste of that pussy first. That's usually how I work, if you don't mind."

Another burst of giggles. "No, I really don't. I'd really like to meet with you as well."

"Okay. Let me have your home address, and tell me when you'd like me to swing by?"

"Well let's see … today's Thursday, how about we make it the weekend, Saturday. I'll be at home all through and you can come by whenever it pleases you. Here's my address; are you ready?"

"Yeah, go ahead." Zee listened as she narrated her address out for him. He told her he would be in touch and for her to save his number in her phone so as to get at him anytime. They exchanged pleasantries before hanging up. His erection hadn't died completely; he was still wired from the sound of her cute voice. He left his chair and went into the bathroom and jerked himself off inside the toilet bowl.

Zee went about his normal business that Thursday night till Friday. His mind shelved off anything that had to do with his impending meeting with Marilyn. It helped him to focus better when he didn't think too seriously of his dates.

By Friday evening when he got back from work, he checked his mail and saw that she'd written to him again. This time she had attached a couple of snapshots of herself. There was one she'd taken some months back while on a holiday trip with her husband down at Yellowstone Park. Her body still looked firm, though not as curvaceous as a woman in her twenties, Zee thought, but who really cared, as long as the pussy's good. She was a mature-looking lady—a cougar in the making. Her hair was thick and flaming red; she had a round face with a splatter of freckles on her arm and shoulder. She had jutting hips with a nice pair of round ass. Ass good enough to smack, he mused. And her tits sure looked plump. The other snapshots (three of them) were of her naked lying on a bed striking different poises; photos had probably been taken by her man, he thought. One of them she was bent over, facing the opposite wall, her hands reaching back to spread her ass cheeks, showing the camera an up-close view of her glistening coochie. What a nice coochie that's got to be, Zee licked his lips in anticipation of what tomorrow would bring. In the mail, she'd written:

Hope you like the pics. There's plenty more where those came from. Can't wait to see you tomorrow.

Lots of love,
Marilyn.

Zee couldn't wait either.

***

Friday morning arrived. He'd called Marilyn informing her he'd be at her doorstep between eleven and noon; he was there in his Range Rover Jeep at 11:37 a.m.

Marilyn's home was a simple brick structure with a well-kept front yard. Zee parked his car beside their driveway and walked towards the front door. He didn't make it in time before the door flew open and there stood Marilyn welcoming him with a brimming smile. She was wearing a knee-length purple bathrobe; Zee wondered if she had any surprises lurking inside it. It wasn't long before he found the answer to that question.

"Nice to finally meet you, Marilyn," he came and embraced her, feeling her ample breasts press against his chest, sending a 'come alive' signal to his crotch. He wore a tight sweat shirt and blue jeans, his desire to get her to acknowledge his physique which evidently she did.

"Nice to meet you too, Zee," she caressed the muscles on his arm. "Hmm, you must really work out."

"As much as I can. A brother's always got to keep fit."

She invited him into her home and closed the door behind him, turning in the key as well. Zee asked about her husband and she told him he'd gone out to get some late shopping and probably won't be back for another hour or two. She would have gone with him, except she just had to attend to Zee's coming over.

"Would you care for something to drink?" she asked him.

"Nah, I'm good for now, thanks."

They sat close to each other on the long sofa. Marilyn raised her robe and folded her legs behind her, her eyes focused on her visitor. Her robe parted slightly to give Zee a good view of her meaty thigh. Zee felt another rise in his crotch; he couldn't wait to feel his hands over the flesh of that thigh.

"You told your man that I'd be coming around today?"

"Oh yeah, he knows. I know he'd like to meet you."

"As long as he doesn't take all day to get the shopping done." He indicated at her robe. "You got anything lurking behind that robe I need to see?"

She smiled and then got up from the couch, standing before him. "Actually I thought you'd never ask." She loosened her robe and let it slip from her arms to reveal her nakedness underneath. She had on a purple thong and black thigh stockings and nothing else. Zee adjusted himself on the couch as he felt the pressure of his cock squirming inside his jeans, begging for its freedom. Marilyn turned around and wiggled her ample-sized bum at him; he nodded his approval at what he saw.

"Nice, very nice. How about you bringing that lovely body of yours over here," he indicated at his lap. "Come sit over big daddy's legs."

Marilyn went to him dutifully. She crossed her legs over his thighs straddling him, as Zee adjusted himself further to make her comfy. Her ass pressed down on the tent that was his crotch while her breasts with their jutting nipples met his face. Zee didn't withhold himself from kissing her tits, hearing her moan as he bit on her right nipple. He grasped her ass, loved the feel of their ample roundness in his hands. "Yeah," he murmured. "You've got a nice ass. I know a lot of brothers are going to love hitting on you."

"Really? You think so? I always thought they looked kind of rumpled and ugly."

"Not from where I'm sitting. Though as your pimp in concern, I'm going to have to test your pussy out. Need to make damn sure your body's just right. Hope you don't mind?"

"Oh sure, I was looking forward to that." she grinned lasciviously. "Can I ask you something?"

"Anything."

"Is it true about that talk that once a white woman goes black, she hardly ever goes back? I keep thinking it's something that sounds kind of bogus."

"Nothing bogus about that, babe. That's the real truth. A good thing too that you're about to find out just how true it is."

She bent her head and kissed him. "Hmmm, I hope you don't mind if I suck your cock first?"

"Hell no I don't."

She climbed off him to the side and watched as he undid his belt buckle and then and pushed his jeans and boxer shorts to his ankle. He extracted his feet from his trainers and jeans and then sat back to give her a better view of what he was packing. Marilyn gasped at the sight of his cock, noted the way it curved an inch towards the right, with the black vein throbbing to the side. By far it was a cock bigger than her husband's and those of her former boyfriends. She came forward and wrapped her fingers around it, feeling its pulsing power travel up her arm like a wave of electric current. *My God, so it's a true what they say about black cocks after all*, she thought to herself, noting the pre-cum fluid that came out of the tiny hole of his cock's bulbous head. Zee relished the look of awe that was on her face. It never ceased to amaze him how a lot of white wives tend to transform once their eyes set of his dick. A good thing it was for him that he was doing what he was doing and loving it.

"Wow, that is a big cock," she confirmed, leaning closer towards it. "I'm getting wet already just from looking at it."

"Then you'd better not keep me waiting, slut." He pushed her head down on his cock.

Marilyn opened her mouth in time and grunted when his cock jammed all the way into her throat. She wrapped her thick lips quickly around it and proceeded to suck it. Zee sighed at the warm, wet presence of her mouth; he kept jamming her head down on his dick, wanting her to suck him faster. He loved nothing like a good blowjob, and a woman who knew very well how to give good head in his opinion was a certified keeper … that included black women, white, Asians, or even alien Martians.

"Yeah, go on and suck that fat cock," he murmured while he pushed her hair off from her face. "I want you to open your jaws up and deep-throat it all the way, and don't come up for air unless you have to."

Marilyn did as he ordered. She let in air into her mouth and then took as much of his cock that she could swallow. She could feel the round head touching against her tonsil. She held it in her mouth for a moment before pulling back off, gasping for breath while she did. She spat on his cock, jerked it a couple of times then returned her head down to it. Her back was bent in a crouch; Zee extended his right arm under her body and rubbed the outward flesh that was her pussy. Marilyn squirmed from his touch, but still she remained her attention on sucking him. Zee held her head and began pumping his hips up, fucking her mouth as he wanted.

"Yeah, I'm gonna teach you how to suck a black cock," he instructed her. "You're gonna learn real good … gonna learn how to become a black man's slut. Going to dress you as one too. Anytime you see a black man walking down the street, the first thing you're going to be thinking about is getting that black cock of his jammed down your throat. That what you want, bitch?"

She gave a muffled grunt.

He smacked her bum and snapped at her. "Answer me, bitch!"

She freed her mouth from his cock and cried out: "Yes! Yes, that's what I want!"

Zee opened his legs further for her to work her mouth on his balls too. When he felt he'd had enough, he pulled her up from his cock and got up. She wasn't too happy about it, but figured it was alright. Zee made her lie back on the couch, pulled her hips forward and pushed her thong to the side so as to sink his lips unto her wet pussy. Marilyn squirmed and gasped abruptly from the contact of his tongue; she took newfound joy with the way it slipped and licked over her clit and wiggled her crotch before him. Zee brought his hands under her ass and pushed it up to get an affordable taste of her pussy and her juice pouring out of it. He was very good at this. His lips slid up and down, perusing her sweet, honey juice through her inner walls, then returning up to nibble on her clit. The sound of her moaning rose and fell like octave music notes in his ears.

Marilyn whimpered breathlessly, her hands squeezing her tits. "Oh my God! Ohhh Zee … Ohhh master! Oh don't stop! I'm gonna … *OHH SHIT! I'M GONNA CUM! I'M GONNA CUMMM!*"

Her body shook all over and she went into a cycle of spasms as she pushed her body up from the couch, but Zee remained in control of the situation and didn't let up from the appalling ecstasy he'd unleashed upon her. Her hands left her tits and pressed down on his head. His lips still remained locked on her clit, his tongue swimming in the sea of her pussy juice as she exploded into orgasm. When finally he pulled off, he left her there to simper in her delight while he wiped her cum off his face with her robe. Marilyn remained where she was gasping. How long it had been since she carved for such an orgasm and here it was. It felt so fantastic she wanted to remain like that to savour the experience. Zee didn't make her wait that long. He knelt by her head and offered her his cock. Marilyn grasped it and sucked it with as much passion her lips could muster.

"You ready to take that cock right now?" he asked her.

"Oh yes, I want it," she moaned as she jerked his shaft. "I want it right now, master."

Zee brought her to lean on the couch facing the wall, feeling his hand over her ample buttocks as he pulled her thong panties down her legs. At that moment there came the rattle of a key in the front door and their heads turned towards it as the door came open and in stepped her husband. Danny was of average height, had a slender frame with wide-staring eyes hiding behind a pair of glasses. He had some packages in his arm and after closing the door and turning to face the naked persons in the room with him; his eyes seemed to nearly bulge out of their sockets at the sight before him. Zee was unfazed by the man disrupting them. Numerous occasions he'd been surprised this way and knew very well how to handle things when they called for it. His erection remained rock hard and throbbing with blood pumping in his veins.

"Hi honey," Marilyn waved at him from where she was. "You're just in time. I'd like you to meet Zee whom I'd told you about. Zee this is Danny, my husband."

"Much obliged," he came forward and shook her husband's hand.

"Likewise," Danny answered. His eyes then gazed down at Zee's cock and once again his eyes took on that bulging outlook. "You … you guys just about to get started. I haven't missed anything, have I?"

"Hell yeah we are," Marilyn answered with glee. "Zee here just made me cum like I've never had before. Now I want you to take a seat and watch, okay honey?"

Danny nodded, dropping the packages by his feet. "I can do that."

"Whoa! Hold on there, white boy," Zee snapped at him, taking charge. "I've got a little work for you to do." He fumbled with one of the pockets of his jeans and unearthed his car keys which he then gave to Danny. "The Range Rover parked outside is mine. Look in the passenger seat you'll find a folder and a digital camera. Fetch them for me, and hurry."

He turned his attention back to Marilyn as Danny dashed out the door. He beat his cock against the smoothness of her ass; Marilyn giggled at the feeling and wiggled her buttocks at him. Zee positioned himself as he found her pussy opening and pushed his cock in-between and heard Marilyn groan a response. Zee took things gently with her as Danny quickly returned with a file folder and a digital camera in hand. Zee took the camera, told him to hold onto the folder, and began taking shots of his thick shaft exiting and disappearing inside Marilyn's ass. He told her to look at him and he took one of her flushed face before dropping the camera by the couch and starting to slam into her hard.

Marilyn hugged the top of the couch and began moaning in rhythm with Zee's large prick fucking her cunt. His dick just seemed to expand even the tiniest space of her pussy hole, each pounding sent shockwaves of excitement coursing up her body. Zee loved the sight of her ass cheeks bouncing forward and then backward each time he slammed into her. His shaft was lathered with her pussy juice when he pulled it out of her. Zee couldn't resist smacking her bum; Marilyn yelped from it. He grabbed a fistful of her hair, pulled her head backwards and went on slamming his cock in her cunt as hard as he could. The sound of her moans rose to high rise shrieks. She too thrust her ass backwards to meet with his cock, crying out her pleasure while she did.

"Oh my God!" she moaned heavily. "Ohh master, that feels so fucking good!"

"You like the way my dick's pounding you, bitch?"

"Uhhhh-yeahhh … I love it! *I FUCKING LOVE IT!*"

"Good, 'cause there's more where that comes from. Come here, bitch. Get your thick ass off that sofa."

He smacked her buttocks one last time as she got to her feet. Zee picked up her robe and spread it on the floor. Danny got up and pushed aside the centre table. Zee gave his camera to Danny, instructing him to take some good snapshots. He lowered himself on her robe and indicated for her to come straddle him. Marilyn crouched on top of his and took his cock and guided it into her pussy. Danny came around and stood behind them, training the camera on his wife's ass and began snapping away. Zee wedged his hands under her meaty thighs and pumped his hips upwards as fast as he could, slapping her cunt with his shaft. Marilyn almost lost her balance in the midst of her excitement. Zee's cock pounded her pussy and she thought she could feel it stabbing at her heart. She brought her legs down and leaned forward with her tits over his face. His hands grabbed a handful of her ass cheeks and fingered her asshole while still pounding her. Danny licked his lips as he bounced around them taking snapshot after snapshot of his wife's pussy gushing out cum juice over the black cock that was fucking her raw. The sound of her cries filled the room, mouthing a hundred expletives while she did.

"Ohh shit! Ohh God! Fuck me! Fuck me good, Zee! … *OOHHH FUCK ME, YOU FUCKER!*"

All the way that she's crying out, her moans coupled with the sound of Zee's thighs smacking rapidly with the underside of her ass. Zee groaned a moment later and reached behind and took his cock out of her pussy. One forced jerk followed by a heavy grunt from him and a stream jet of semen shot out of the head of his cock like lightning and splattered over the backside of Marilyn's ass. He went on groaning and jerking more spurts of sperm onto the back of her ass cheeks till he shot his last load. Marilyn collapsed on top of him. Some of his thick semen rolled down the crack of her ass and dripped over the now swollen meaty glands of her pussy. Danny leaned forward and took careful snapshots; his eye didn't miss a thing.

Marilyn rolled off him, still gasping. Zee came to his knees and positioned his cock beside her face. Marilyn took his shaft that was now wet with his cum and her pussy juice into her mouth. Some of his cum dripped down her chin as she licked her tongue down his shaft, moaning in her mouth while she did. Zee told her to hold her poise and indicated at Danny to come closer and take a snapshot of her rubbing her tongue against his shaft. Danny did as was told, fixed his eye on the view lens and pressed down on the shutter, taking not one snapshot but three.

"Perfect!" he announced. He took a step back and took a last shot of Zee bent over his wife with her hand still cradling his cock; how they looked so good with each other.

"Just fucking perfect," he said again.

***

Marilyn led Zee into their bathroom to clean up, while Zee opened the folder her husband had retrieved from his vehicle and took out a contractual agreement he'd drafted months ago when he started his pimping network and gave it to Danny to read through. There wasn't much fancifulness of legalistic grammar in the document. It stated in clear language that the above named housewife/woman would be under his pimping tutelage under a starting duration of two months with no monetary exchange involved. If at the end of the indicated time frame, should the couple desire extract themselves from the contract then they're more than willing to do so without any hassle. However should they still wish to retain his pimping connections, then a second contractual agreement would be drawn for that. There were two identical copies—one for the hubby and the other for the pimp's keep—and for the hubby to sign both.

Danny went into the kitchen and sat at the kitchen table, read through the one-page fine print while Marilyn and Zee remained busy soaping and playing in the shower. She couldn't stop chattering to him about how overwhelmed she was when he'd made her cum. The experience was overwhelming, one she never thought she'd have again as it has been so long. Zee did some pitching, told her not to worry that by the time he'd spread her around the clubs and neighbourhoods she would be having such orgasms on a daily basis just from thinking about getting fucked by a black dick. Marilyn loved the sound of his voice whenever he mentioned 'black dick'. She especially loved the slutty words he'd used on her when they'd been fucking. She said it made her feel very dirty.

While they talked under the shower her hand never let go of Zee's cock. She held unto it like it was a desired appendage—very desirable for her—and wished she'd been getting so much of it prior to today. Obviously today was one day she never was going to make herself forget.

Zee drew her towards him and planted his tongue into her lips. The kiss was long and passionate; Marilyn let herself surrender to him once again. Zee's hands caressed her ass cheeks, fondled it and then smacked it, loving the sound it made when his palms made contact. He knew she wanted another round, and the good thing was he was getting aroused to give her another. He was here to test her pussy out after all and that was what he intended to do. So unfortunate he couldn't use the entire day for that.

They finished showering and towelled themselves dry and stepped out of the bathroom. Zee made her get on the bed, had her assume the exact position of being on her arms and knees with her so fine-looking white bum and gaping pussy presenting itself to him. He lowered his face and licked his way through her pussy's lips like he'd done earlier. Marilyn rested her head on her arms, moaning softly. Her ass wiggled up and down and then around in time with his sucking. Her juice gushed down on his face like a faucet; still Zee was unmindful and went on licking her clit.

He pulled his face off from between her ass cheeks, not wanting to do her as much as he'd earlier done, then came forward and thrust his cock into her awaiting hole. His cock slid into her with very little effort. Though her pussy still felt a bit tight, Zee couldn't help but grit his teeth from the sensation. He pushed his shaft all the way inside her, fucking her cunt as hard as he could. Marilyn in no time was groaning back hard from his pounding. Her eyes were half shut, savouring the feel of his shaft slamming inside her while her tits jiggled under her chest.

Zee pulled out and turned her over to lie on her back. He spread her legs further apart as she reached for his cock and shoved it back inside her. His fingers rubbed on her clit and fingered her pussy as well. Marilyn howled with delight as further shockwaves seared across her body. A moment later she was panting with fervour; her tits bounced and wiggled like half-filled water balloons. It wasn't long before she cried herself to another orgasm. Zee remained hard inside of her, still hammering her with his cock till he felt the sensation of the trigger-pull building at the tip of his cock. He was tempted to flood her with his semen, but figured it was much too early for that. Instead he retrieved his cock, hopped on the bed and began pumping his shaft. He groaned aloud when jet stream of semen shot out of his cock and splattered over Marilyn's tits and face.

He slumped to the side of the bed breathing heavy, his cock gradually growing flaccid. Marilyn turned over and reached for his cock, cleaning the stream of cum that lathered his shaft. Zee couldn't help but smile; she sure was going to make a good slut.

She paused in her sucking and glanced up at him and smiled. "You like how I'm sucking your cock, Zee?"

"Yeah, I sure do. Keep on like this, and you're going to be going places real soon. Going to run a train through that pussy of yours."

"What do you mean by 'run a train'?"

"It means that I'm going to get a couple of brothers to do a gangbang job on you. You think you're going to be up for that?"

She made her face as if to consider it. "Well, I don't really know. I've never done two before, though I've always wanted to try it."

"You will, honey. Trust me, you will."

"I already do, darling." She returned her head down to sucking him.

They snuggled in each other's arms for a while. Zee played with her tits, kissing and biting each nipple while she lay in submission under him. He was soon getting hard again. Damn, he wanted to screw her one more time but he had more business to take care of in town. Such was a temptation too hard for him to pass. Just lying here groping her ass was enough to recharge his batteries. He ought to have made her give him a titty-fuck. Oh well, next time's always a charm. They showered once more; Marilyn was just as sad to hear he had to leave for something else. She went to the living room to fetch his clothes and he put them on while at the same time watcher her scurry her butt into a pair of tight shorts. They returned downstairs to Danny who'd finished reading through the contract document with his signature at the bottom. Zee took his copy while the husband kept his.

"Hope you took your time about it," Zee asked him. "Last thing I want is getting late night phone calls asking about where your woman is, so I hope you took the whole shit seriously."

"I understand everything, Mr. Zee. Anything that's going to do fine for Marilyn is all right with me. Obviously she'll be with better company with you."

Marilyn kissed her husband's cheek. "That's so nice of you, honey. Really, thanks."

"Think nothing of it, sweetheart." Danny returned the affectionate kiss.

Before he left, he exchanged phone numbers and email addresses with him, saying that he would be in touch with Marilyn as soon as he'd set up her snapshots on his web page. The couple walked with him to his car. He shook Danny's hand and gave Marilyn a peck and squeezed her bottom too.

"I'll call you later tonight," she said to him. They waved at him as he started his car and turned it into a reverse and drove out of the neighbourhood.

***

Fifteen minutes later Zee pulled into a Dunkin' Donuts rest stop to feed himself. He hadn't realised just how famished he was until he'd driven off from Marilyn's home. All that hot sexual energy he'd expended while having fun with that pussy was now biting at his stomach walls. He checked his watch; it said 3:35 p.m. Time sure ran fast when you're having fun. He thought back on Marilyn and wondered how big her kids were. If they were past eighteen, that would be cool. If such then maybe he could sway her into getting them involved in the business. He'd always dreamed of having a mother and daughter on his pimp roll; and if the hubby's the type that would enjoy cleaning the wife's cunt as well as black brother's cocks when they were done cumming, then there's no way that shouldn't work. enough of that for now, he thought to himself as he pulled into the Dunkin' Donuts' parking lot and went inside to make his order. He carried his food tray to an empty booth and decided to make a call first. To his next scheduled date.

A woman's voice came to the line. "Hello?"

"Hi Crystal. It's Zee on the line."

"Oh hi Zee! Gosh, I was wondering when I'd get to see you. Aren't you coming by my place again?"

"Sure I'm going to be there. That's actually the reason why I'm calling. I got held up someplace with work I needed to take care of."

"I hope you're not dodging me today, are you?"

"Now why would you want to go think something nasty like that? I won't ever think of dodging you. I just had some important things to take care of, but I'll be at your door soon enough."

"I hope you do. When you said you'd be coming over today, I went out earlier in the day and bought myself a lovely yellow dress. It's a real killer tight outfit. I'd really like you to see it when you get here."

"You've been a naughty girl lately, haven't you, Crystal?"

The sound of her laughter bounced in his ear. "You should know I was always naughty before you met me. Besides, I know you like me that way."

"I most certainly do. You really know how to make a brother hard without making him sweat." The tingling sensation in his crotch was alerting his cock to salacious thoughts. "I can't wait to fuck you in your new outfit. Just don't think of going anywhere until I get there."

"Wasn't ever dreaming of doing that. Where are you right now?"

"I'm at a Dunkin' Donuts right now getting my swerve on."

"You could have come straight down and saved your money, I would have cooked you some grub."

"I know, babe, and I'm sorry but the work I'd been doing really sapped a lot of energy off me. I'll have a couple of bites then I'm start hurrying over."

"Better not keep me waiting all day, Zee?" she stressed. "Really I'm aching for you right now."

I'll bet you are, Zee thought and smiled to himself before saying goodbye to her and continuing with his meal.

It was a well-earned pride to his ego that he could so easily take any upstanding white woman in the city and within a matter of hours or days turn her into the last thing any white man would ever expect her to be—a 'let's-go-crazy' slut. Few had stood against his charms and walked away from him; others though they'd looked at him with abhorrence at his suggestions had afterwards searched him out whether online or at the numerous night clubs he frequented. Even though he successfully pimped them out to sometimes earn money for him while they did it for kicks, they never tired from wanting a piece of him every now and then to sort of recharge their batteries after being driven by other hungry black cocks out there. Zee too was always ready to oblige their insatiable want. After all, he belonged to them just as much as they too relied so much on him.

While he consumed his meal, his eyes, having nothing better to do, roamed around, observing the people coming in and leaving, ogling the few pretty females seated close to him the way a lion would scout a grassland in search of a hapless prey standing out from the crowd. It was the right kind of place to pick and scoop out chicks, most especially the lonesome ones. Some of them were here too in search of a hook-up but seldom realised it.

It was in such a similar place he'd bumped into Crystal.

He and several of his buddies had driven to a snack house after a friendly B' ball game when he'd noticed her alone with herself at a corner booth, looking so fine with no one for company. Zee wasn't the sort to let a fine moment like the one he had then pass him by, thus he'd sauntered over to her table, sat down and they'd struck up a conversation while neglecting his friends who'd gone along without him. It hadn't taken long for her to open herself to him. She had recently broken up with her husband. He'd found himself a younger companion to be with and chucked her to the curb. This was all a month ago. Crystal was a long-haired blonde, a few years shy of turning forty. Zee hadn't moved in on her till about a week, giving her time to get over her divorce headache. They'd spent an evening at a club, feeling the heat as they danced so close, their lips connected while their hands fondled each other's body. She'd dedicated herself towards pleasing black cocks since then, starting with his, then moving on to more aggressive ones. The bigger or thicker the black cock, the better. Zee reckoned her former hubby had done the right thing leaving her for a younger slut for him to scoop up and remould into what she was now. Crystal had never been with a black person before in her life prior to when she met Zee. But that had changed less than a week later; Zee had made damn sure of that.

Like his other working women in the city, Zee had set up an online blog page for her, and fastidiously pimped her about to fellas in need of some desperate white pussy to fuck, and steadily her page had been getting more and more hits. Lots of white hubbies loved stopping by to watch her numerous erotic videos while he'd taped that featured her fucking different brothers, or a multitude of them.

Zee paused in his reverie and looked up with his half-finished burger that was in his hand. Some woman was giving him the cute eye. She sat five tables in front of him. She wasn't alone, but from the look of things, the guy she was with seemed to be boring her.

Nothing Zee could do about—he had to respect the guy's game, even though he was making a fool of himself. Besides, he hadn't the time. He finished his meal, gave her a parting wink as he got up and made his way out of the place. Walking to his car, he stopped and turned, making like he was looking for something and caught another good glimpse of the woman through the window. In that brief moment in time, their eyes locked on each other's. Zee gave her a smile before jumping into his car and then pulling out of the space.

He'd just had himself a good meal, but he knew a much better one awaited him at Crystal's place.

***

He made the drive in nine minutes, pulling into her driveway just as the city's heat was mellowing down. Crystal had been anticipating his arrival and she stepped out of her home to welcome him, wearing the yellow evening dress she'd told him about on the phone. The dress hugged and brought out ever curve in her body including her tits, Zee noticed as he killed his car's engine and sized her up. She looked like something good enough to eat. He alighted from his car and she wrapped her arms around his neckline and they kissed.

"Hello, my black prince," she murmured.

Zee laughed. "You're spoiling me with sweet words, Cris."

"You deserve it and more."

She led him into the house—the one she'd won from the custody battle with her ex after the divorce papers had been signed. They sat next to each other on a thick sofa. She crossed one pair of leg over his, her dress parted to reveal her inner thigh and the fact that she hadn't no panties on.

"I've been waiting all day for you to show," she said to him.

"I know. Like I said, I had some other stuff to take care of. I had little time to get away."

22

"Well, all's forgiven now that you're here. So, what do you thing?" she indicated at the dress.

Zee nodded his head approvingly. "You're looking real hot, ma'am. What's the occasion – got yourself a hot date lined up for tonight that I don't know about?"

She slapped his arm playfully. "The only date I've got lined up for today is you and no one else but. Though you're going to have to make it up to me for being late. Hope you got yourself something large to eat on the way."

"Oh yeah," he patted his mid-section. "I'm quite heavy right now."

"Good," she pulled his head towards hers and kissed his lips. "Because you've got to pleasure me before I let you go today."

Zee reached his arm over to pulled her towards him. Crystal came over and sat astride his thighs. His hands raised the back of her dress and he grasped and caressed her bare ass; his finger rubbed between her ass cheeks and dug into her ass crack. Crystal quivered from his touch and laughed at the same time ground herself against him as his finger rubbed against the tiny aperture that was her asshole. Her hands ran over his head and face as she then brought her lips down upon his. She was hungry for him. Zee felt lucky that he'd taken enough grub to replenish the strength he'd left back at Marilyn's place. Obviously he was going to require a lot of it to satisfy this hungry mature slut he was with.

Crystal pulled down the arms of her yellow dress and her jutting breasts with their perfect tan lines bounced before his face. Zee sucked on her left breasts and squeezed the other while she moaned openly at the same time ran her hands over his head. Her body tightened and she muttered a squeal as his finger slipped inch after inch into her anal hole and she went on grinding her hips over the impressive bulge in his crotch.

"Looks like somebody wants to pop out of your jeans to have some fun," she cooed. "Would you want me to take care of him for you?"

"In a little while," Zee groaned. "Got to take care of you first."

He turned to his side and laid her on the sofa. She held up her dress as he came downward between her open legs and licked his tongue up and down the rich pink lips that was her pussy. Crystal's breathing came in stuttering gasps and opened her legs further and raised her hips for Zee's tongue to probe her cunt.

"Ohh God ... Oh Zee! Go on, lick me good!" she moaned on and on. "Go on, lick my pussy. Then when you're done, I want you to take me upstairs and fuck me like a whore! Will you do that for me, darling?"

Zee paused in his licking. "Oh yeah. I'll fuck you like you're the dirtiest whore I ever laid eyes on."

He burrowed his face between the light growth of blonde hair growing in her pubic region like a rabbit digging for treasure and Crystal could do nothing but lie there with her hands holding back her legs taking the striking swirl of pleasure he was meting on her. She beat her head side to side on the sofa's arm rest; her crotch undulated against Zee's probing tongue, wanting more from it. Her body went through spasms and she gave a whimpered cry as a flood of orgasm washed over her. Crystal remained as she was until the storm had quietened down before she then stood up, pulling him to his feet and undid his belt and buttons of his jeans with itching fingers. Her lips salivated almost instantly as she took sight of his cock and she pushed his jeans down his thighs to get full view of his erection.

"So black and beautiful," she ran her tongue over her lips.

She didn't need anyone telling her what to do. Crystal brought her face forward immediately and wrapped her lips around the tip of his prick. She had her fingers wrapped around his throbbing meat and sucked stroked his shaft at the same time; her mouth made smacking sounds while she did. She took turns with sucking him and then deep-throating his meat. She had graduated from Zee's tutelage of deep-throating and every time they were together she always loved to show-off her skills for him. Zee held his breath intermittently but it wasn't enough to stop him from groaning at her actions. He already had plans of introducing her to any latest slut he was recruiting so she could help coach them too in how to handle prospective clients with their mouths. Nothing would profit better than a lot of younger sluts having older mentors such as Crystal to pass on what they've learnt about how to please black men.

"Don't forget my balls too, slut!" Zee said to her.

Crystal replied with her actions, holding his thick shaft to the side and pulling at his balls with her mouth one testicle at a time. The action drove Zee up the wall, gasping through gritted teeth.

"*GADDAMN, GIRL!* Your mouth's got me thinking bitchy thoughts right now."

"Hmmm … I love it when you call me a bitch," she murmured.

"Yeah, you're my perfect bitch, you bee-aitch! Love a bee-aitch who loves sucking my cock the way you are."

She choked her mouth on his shaft and then pulled out, stroking his shaft. "You going to fuck me hard with this big cock of yours, darling?"

"Oh hell yeah, I'm gonna bang up your pussy real good. Gonna give your cunt the banana splits by the time I'm done with it. You want me to do that to you, bitch?"

"Ohh yeah!" she moaned. "I want you to fuck me hard and make me cum over and over, darling."

"That's my girl." He pressed her head down on his cock. "Yeah, go ahead … suck that cock, you dirty bitch, slut. Suck it like you've never sucked a black cock ever in your life!"

They always loved it when he talked dirty with them. Seldom was there any white woman who upon becoming addicted to black cock could stand being in entrenched in former pristine lifestyle they'd always felt among with their white male counterparts. Most can't see themselves being a part of that lifestyle anymore, even though they sometimes had to pretend about it just so to keep being accepted by the society around them. With Crystal, she loved been treated and fucked dirty like a slut. That had only progressed with time when he'd begun with her. Things had at first been touch and go, but that period now ancient history. Zee reckoned if her former man came by right now and saw her sucking his cock like she was right now, he'd be mighty pressed to want her back; it brought a smile to his lips. Crystal caught the look in his eye and stopped for a moment.

"You thought up something funny?" she asked.

"I was just wondering what your ex would think if he walked in here right now and saw you sucking me like a pro."

"Fuck him," she said dismissively as she resumed her sucking. "I'd kick his ass if ever he came by here."

"Yeah, I'll bet you will."

He held his cock before her face and shoved it in and out of her mouth hard, watching her slobber over his shaft. She was attempting to make him cum, but Zee had other plans. He pulled her up to her feet and let her dress fall from her legs and together they went in the direction of the main bedroom which was up the stairs.

As they approached the foot of the stairwell, Zee held her back, bent her over so that she was touching the second climb of the stairs and rubbed the head of his dick against her wet pussy opening before thrusting it into her. Crystal grabbed hold of the banister and cried sharply as his cock pushed its way into her womb. It did hurt, but it quickly gave way to a pleasurable feeling. Zee held her by her hips and began firing away his hard ammo inside her; the sound of his hips slamming against the underside of her ass felt like thunderclaps. Crystal's blonde hair fell over her head and face, though it did little to suppress the spirited moans she was having. She gave an excited yelp each time Zee pounded her pussy with impunity.

"Oh-yeah! … Ohh-yeah! … *OHH DARLING! … FUCK! FUCK ME!*"

He grabbed a fistful of her hair and pulled her face to the side to look at her. Her face squeezed into a mask of pain and ecstasy while her lips formed an 'O' shape each time she howled. Only when Zee paused to catch his breath did he pull himself to a stop. Crystal pressed her ass backward against his crotch at the same time squeezed her pussy muscles against his shaft. This sent a quiver of excitement up Zee's body; he couldn't help but gasp and mutter 'Damn!'

Her hands reached behind and held unto him from behind just as he too squeezed her tits against her chest, both of them panting for breath. They struggled to make their way up the stairs, neither wanting to let go of the other. When they got halfway up the stairs, Zee stopped her held up one of her legs over the balustrade, took aim of her pussy with his cock as if aiming for the bulls-eye and then drove it home. Crystal welcomed the feel of him inside her again with a yearning moan, and once more he was back to slamming all solid inches of his cock inside her. Crystal held unto the balustrade as if for dear life. A tremor was searing through her abdomen signalling an incoming orgasm. She reached a hand behind and grabbed hold of his arm; Zee noted the signs and held his breath and quickened his pounding. Her hands came and wrapped around the balustrade and she gave a loud cry that seemed to come from deep down her guts as Zee's pounding brought her to climax.

"*OHHHH-OOOHHHH! OHH GOD … GIVE IT TO ME, ZEE! OHHH SHEEETTTTT!!*"

Zee felt as if his own heart was about to explode any minute. Less than ten seconds after Crystal climaxed, he too groaned aloud and came with a bang. They leaned against the balustrade to catch their breaths; Zee couldn't believe with the tremendous bout of fucking he'd just had that he was still standing on his feet.

Crystal too was breathing heavy; she looked down at her legs and saw his cum dripping down her thighs.

"Uhh … Uhhh my … my God! Ohh God! That was smashing," she murmured.

Zee carried her into his arms as if she were paperweight and took her into the bedroom.

***

The sun's rays were the colour of deep orange as the evening approached and it gradually went down in the sky. Crystal snuggled against her pimp, rubbing her nose and lips against his chin. Under the covers she took his hand and placed it between her thighs; her thighs still bore evidence of their fucking, as it was coated with Zee's cum. He gave her thigh a gentle squeeze, getting a vibe of the heat that lady further up her legs. She turned his head away from staring at the ceiling and kissed him. Always her heart ached like crazy whenever he was around. Being around Zee was like having a permanent rock in her life. It had been a long time since she ever ran into someone as caring about her like he was. The thought was losing him seldom played on her mind.

They'd had hot raunchy sex for almost an hour before calling it quits. Zee lay on the soft quilt of her bed while Crystal rested her head upon his shoulder. The windows were open, but the air wasn't breezy enough to sweep away the sweet smell of cum mixed with their dry sweat. Neither of them was willing to get up yet. For both rounds that they had fucked, Zee had exploded his rich and copious load of semen inside Crystal's cunt. Unlike Marilyn who was a first-timer, Zee always liked cumming inside his women, and they too loved it. For Crystal she just couldn't get enough of it, though she as well loved it whenever she had to swallow his load. Had Zee met her while she'd still been married, he would have known that her number one favourite fantasy was having her worthless husband be there to watch a black stud fuck her and use her like a slut and then cum inside her and for her then to kneel over her hubby's face and let the black man's cum pour over him into his awaiting mouth. "That really would have got me going each time I remember that I'm no longer married to his fucking ass," she'd explained to Zee. "Just the thought of knowing that he too had swallowed your cum like a little bitch would crack me up."

"For you, I'd make sure he ate my nuts every time," he said.

"Thank you, darling," she said to him. "You've got some place else you're supposed to be at right now?"

"Not with the little strength I've got left. No, from here it is home, and once my door closes I'm not setting foot outside of it till morning."

She felt a pang of disappointment in her heart. "Aww, and I was hopping you'd spend the night, keep me company."

"Hold on, I thought you were having company over tonight."

"I told you I wasn't, silly you," she pouted. "I never invite anyone down here once I know you're coming around."

"You could have mentioned earlier that you wanted me to stay. I'd love to stay but I've got some stuff to take care of back at my place."

"Such as?"

He shook his head. "Boring stuff."

"You've got some girl there waiting for you, isn't it?" she said with a touch of jealousy.

"Don't act like that, Criss. You know how much I hate it when you start acting like that."

She curled against his arm. "I'm sorry. It's been a while since I had you to myself; I'm afraid of losing you."

"So far that ain't happened, babe."

"Or that you not wanting me anymore."

"When and whatever gave you that idea?"

Crystal simply shrugged as an answer, giving him a pair of sad eyes.

"Listen girl, I'm not your former man. That guy was an asshole leaving you for some young tramp he'd just met. You're a full woman, and you're my number one girl. Stop putting stuff in your head that don't ought to be there, okay."

She saw the sincerity in his eyes and melted from it. "Okay Zee, darling. I'm sorry for acting like a bitch."

"You're my favourite white bitch," he smiled and then kissed her. "Don't ever sweat the bad vibes, girl. Just pass them off to someone else or throw them away. But don't ever let them sweat you to get you down."

"You're right, I shouldn't. Thanks for being my rock."

Zee couldn't have been any happier. As a pimp, it was his duty to apply soothing words where other brothers would have answered with a fist. He was well adept with his women's emotions and knew what buttons to press to get them turned back to his frequency.

"It'll soon be dark," Crystal murmured against his chest. "I hate being alone in this house without you in it. I get so lonely that way."

"I thought Elroy was going to keep you company this weekend?"

Elroy was one of her frequent black studs whom Zee had introduced her to; he was a high-baller who loved his money just as much as he enjoyed fucking white sluts on the side. Crystal didn't like him that much, always complained of how irritating he often was with her and she wrinkled her nose when Zee brought up his name.

"He said he'd be out of town this weekend. I didn't press him for when he'd be back."

"Too bad, you should have done that. He's got good credit with me."

"I don't like him that well. The guy's too full of himself, and he keeps acting like i'm some property to him."

"Brothers tend to act silly sometimes, I'll admit to that. But he's got a good dick, ain't he?" he countered.

Crystal laughed and slapped his arm. "Zee! You're so crazy to think that!"

"Yeah, but that was what you said the first time after I'd introduced you to him, wasn't it? You talked about it afterwards, remember?"

"Yeah, I did. But yours is still the one I need all the time. So what do you say? Gonna stay the night with me?"

Zee fell silent for a moment, thinking. Then he said: "Instead of being here, how about you bringing your fine ass over to my place?"

***

The sky had gotten dark more than an hour later when they were both dressed up and ready to leave. Crystal was back in her yellow dress with nothing else underneath, carrying her over-night bag with her. She parked her Lincoln in the garage and locked up the house; she opted to take a cab home in the morning. Zee excused himself to make a few phone calls. He hadn't planned on spending the night with her, but now he was, had to redo his evening schedule. He called up a fresh hot pussy whom he'd caught recently, Myra, and explained the situation of things for her that she should drop by his pad tomorrow morning and not tonight anymore. His cock was going to be well fed before the night was over.

They arrived at his condo sometime later. Crystal remarked about liking his new set of curtains compared to the former one as he let her into his home. She went towards his bedroom to freshen up while Zee emptied his pockets on the centre table along with the signed copy of the agreement Marilyn's husband had signed. He took off his jeans and threw it lazily on his couch and went to his library room and booth up his computer and printer, bringing along his camera. He opened up a separate file folder in his pictures section and downloaded Marilyn's photos into the folder

31

before logging into first his website: www.pimpersparadise.com, and then his blog: Blackmastershango.com.

He spent the next forty minutes working on setting up a profile page for his latest acquisition in his website; for the blog, he uploaded several of her photos and wrote several paragraphs of his time spent with her, as well as a scanned copy of her signed pimp agreement. He wanted other hubbies and wives who frequented both his blog and website to be aware of his activities. Some of them had gotten in touch with him wanting to be a part of his growing clientele, others he need desired more pictorial persuasions. Others were brothers who too were in hungry need of white bitches to fuck. He knew just how to whet their appetites. He would finish posting the blog and updating his web page today, then tomorrow he would advertise Marilyn's snapshots at numerous interracial and cuckold forum sites he regularly visited in search of fresh sluts or hubbies wanting the same done to their wives.

This was the new and improved means of pimping, Zee thought to himself. Gone is the old-school style of 70's pimping where a Cadillac brother's got his women pounding the street pavement every day of the week under cold, rain or even sleet, just working her ass off tricking for clients to get him his paper. Ain't no chance in hell Zee was going to roll like that. There's a lot of ways one can handle his business that don't mean one letting his girls trick for him on the street. Nowadays with technology still on the rise, you either make shit work for you, or you pretend it doesn't exist and keep living like one stuck in the Stone Age. This way he could rake in all the dough he needed sometimes without having to step out his door for the day. A lot of brothers who were his clients were trustworthy enough not to dick him around. A good thing he always matched their request regarding what particular sort of white slut they wanted: somewhere right now a brother wanted to mark his birthday and needed a white bitch just to kick the night off. Zee was ready to make shit happen for them with nothing more than a simple phone call. That was just how good he'd set up his piece of paradise for himself.

He was uploading the last of Marilyn's photos unto her own web page when he noticed a shadow behind him. He looked behind his shoulder and there was Crystal wearing one of his NBA tee shirts with her sexy long legs sticking out from under it. She was eating something from a bowl in her hand.

"What do you have there with you?" he asked her.

"Cereal." She answered while taking a spoon to her mouth, and then indicated at what he was doing. "She a new one you found?"

"Yeah she is. Stopped by her crib to give her an interview and then took some snapshots."

"She looks hot."

Crystal came and stood beside him, admiring one of the photos that had him feeding her with his cock. Though the picture only showed him from his waist down, Crystal knew without a doubt that it was him; he had done the same with her the first time they fucked. Though she couldn't help sensing the earlier pang of jealousy creep into her heart and mind again. To fight against it, she dropped her bowl on his table and came and stood behind him, massaging the muscles of his shoulder.

"Was she a good fuck?"

Zee smiled, catching the hint of jealousy in her voice. "If you're asking whether I'm taking you off my mind because of her, you're wrong." He took her hand and made her come and sit over his lap. "This woman is just business."

"And what am I then? Another piece of white meat?"

"You're no white meat to me, Criss. You're my number one girl, remember?"

She pouted. "Yeah, and I'll bet you say that to all your other gir—"

Zee stopped her mouth with a kiss before she could go any further. It was all Crystal desired. She opened her lips to accept his kiss, wrapping her hands around his neck while their lips remained locked on each other's. *Women*, he mused. *No matter how much love, big-dick fucking, or money you give them, still they ain't ever satisfied.*

She came down from his lap; the hungriness for him was back in her eyes. Zee pushed his chair backwards as she knelt before him, tugging his boxers from his waistline just as his erection was nodding awake from its sleep mode. Crystal held his shaft and licked her tongue along its underside before engulfing her mouth on it. She held onto his thighs while her head bobbed up and down on his shaft, bringing him to full erection. He was groaning from the magnetic pull of her mouth when his phone began to ring. He leaned forward and picked it up from his table where he'd left it and said 'hello' into the mouthpiece; he tried hard not to wince from Crystal's oral punishment.

"Hi Zee, good evening," a sultry female voice cooed into his ear. Zee shut his eyes and concentrated on the owner of the voice—Crystal's tongue and lips made it a bit hard for him to do so. Finally it came to him.

"Oh hi there Marilyn … eh, how's the evening being for you?"

"Not too bad. My husband Danny and I ordered some Chinese to sort of celebrate how today went. He's online right now checking out your website and he's seen my snapshots you unloaded and he's going crazy about them right now."

"That's good knowing the white boy likes what he sees. Now a lot of other people out there are going to see more of you."

"I'm so excited about it. Anyway, he wanted me to ask how soon you'll be dropping again."

"I'll be there day after tomorrow … yes, day after tomorrow." I covered the mouthpiece with his hand and groaned through his teeth, fighting back the urge of warmth Crystal's mouth was doing to him. She looked at him with her large pair of eyes smiling at the torture he was on-going. She paused to grin her teeth at him then sunk her mouth once again on his cock, going down as farther as she could.

Zee returned to his phone call. "So, Marilyn, I'll be …Uhhh … stopping by to drop your old man's copy of the contract stuff, and then you're going to have … Uhh … you're going to have yourself a lot of hits on my web page. You got any high glass 'fuck me' pumps to wear?"

"Yeah … yeah, I think I might have somethin—"

"If you don't have one," Zee interrupted her, "then it'll be best if Danny goes out and gets you a pair 'cause you're going to be needing it pretty soon, girl. Or maybe when I drop by your end day after tomorrow we'll see about that." He winced and took the phone farther from his face and groaned once more when Crystal nibbled for long the foreskin of his balls, making him jump in his seat. Crystal loved his reaction and it encouraged her to keep doing it. Zee brought the phone back to his ear, surprised that Marilyn was still at the other end of the line.

"Zee, are you still there?"

"Yeah … yes, I'm here, babe, but can't be on for long. I want you and Danny to go out tomorrow and let him get you some slutty gear, anything you and him can lay your hand on, okay? I'm going to give a call to some brothers later to see if they'd like to break you off. I'll bet that's what you'd like right now, right?"

"Oh yes, that and some more."

"That's my girl. You just go get yourself some sleep now, okay. I'll be talking …" he paused to mutter a gasp. "Uhhh … yeah, as I was saying, go get yourself some rest … I'll talk to you tomorrow."

"Okay Zee. I can hardly wait, and thanks for everything … and for today as well. I really enjoyed everything about today."

"Yeah … me too. Don't you worry, we've got lots more fun to do in time. You go to bed and think happy … happy dreams. Good night."

He cut the line before she could say anything else. He let his phone slip from his hand, gasping. He had to force his cock from Crystal's hands before she would let go of him.

"You're gonna let me cum just like that?" he said to her.

She gave him a sly wink. "Don't look at me, you were the one busy talking on the phone to care about what I was doing." She leaned forward and gave his cock's bulbous head a kiss, and then: "Who was that anyway?"

"A wrong number," he replied.

"You trying to be funny with me, mister?"

"Who's been funny when you've got half of my cock in your mouth."

"Well that's not all that this girl here wants." She got to her feet and pulled his tee shirt off from her head, standing before him naked smiling. "This girl wants to get her pussy wet and fucked deep and hard by your cock. The question is are you up to the task, mister?"

Zee shot to his feet and pulled her up. "You watch me and see, you bitch."

He held her hand and roughly pulled her towards the direction of his bedroom.

***

Zee got dressed and left his apartment a few minutes before ten. Although his appointment wasn't supposed to take place for another two hours—Zee always did his business by the clock—but he had no choice than to leave early. Crystal barely gave him enough room to sleep last night. He'd pounded and pounded her pussy tirelessly and made her cum to her satisfaction. This morning she'd woken him up first with a solid blowjob and then had jumped on top of him with a vengeance. They had fucked steadily for another hour before they unanimously called a 'time-out' when they both became too hungry to continue. He'd left her there, claiming he was in a hurry. It was a good thing he'd gotten dressed while she was at the kitchen making breakfast and told her he had some things to take care of and had to leave right away. He reckoned if he stuck around for breakfast, she was going to be horny once again.

His stomach was growling like a motherfucker while he drove out of his neighbourhood of Frisco Beach heading towards the city. He needed to be at one of his women's place by noon. Some guy had put in a request at his website three days ago about throwing a little house party with several of his fellas and they needed a white nymph to grace the occasion. Zee had just the right slut in mind for the job—Minx. That's a hot slut who could fuck a heard of charging water buffalos to stupor if required. Zee had written back to the fellow wanting to know if his so-called party gang were still interested in the hook-up. The answer had been a yes. A time and place of address had been sent before Zee had made the phone call to Minx, and as expected, her answer too had been a solid yes. The world sure felt right today.

But that was for later—Zee still enough time to burn. First thing he needed to do was fill up his stomach.

He thought about the MacDonald's restaurant he'd eaten at yesterday. He recalled the sight of the pretty pair of eyes of the white girl who'd admired him then and wondered if by some miracle that restaurant was a favourite spot of hers and that he might catch her there sometime again. It was a long shot gamble … but who really knows.

The sky was emitting languorous groans and within a space of minutes was completely covered by thick grey clouds that unleashed a downpour on the city. Zee was just pulling into the MacDonald's restaurant and parking his ride into a just vacated space when the rain became heavy. He opened his door and after locking it hurried as fast as he could into the building. He found himself a table with a window view of the building's front and almost right away a waitress arrived to take his order. He was in the middle of his meal when his phone rang—it was from one of his clients wanting to make a request. He was in the middle of the phone conversation when to his surprise the mystery girl whom he'd been thinking about walked into the building.

Zee kept on his phone conversation while his eyes admired the sight that was before him.

She stood there with her back facing the restaurant's glass doors, wiping rain water from her hair and slapping droplets off her jacket and jeans. Her eyes roamed the room and they stopped when they caught Zee staring at her. Immodesty made her turn her face away and she got herself a table close to the doorway. Zee finished his call then resumed eating his meal while his eyes kept staring at her direction. When he was done, he got up and without thought went towards her table. She was munching on a plate of French fries and sipping a Diet Coke when he came to her table. Her eyes came up and looked at him as he stood in front of her.

"Hi there," he indicated at the spare chair of her table. "Mind if sit here?"

She sized him up with her pair of gorgeous green eyes. "Whatever would you want to sit there for?"

Zee smiled at her. "Was wondering if maybe I could make conversation with you while you eat. That a crime?"

"Not a crime," she tried to hide a blush starting to glow on her cheeks. "But it's very unusual you'd walk all this way to do that. I'm not that good with making conversations."

"My bad," he said, planting himself on the chair. "I'm here for something else anyway."

"Really?" she scooped from French fries into her mouth. "What about?"

"It's like this, I was here yesterday and I could have sworn that you were here too, except you weren't alone like you are today."

"What makes you think it was me you saw here yesterday?"

"Yours isn't the sort of face one would easily forget," he smiled at her. "Especially with those lovely green eyes of yours."

The smile that came to her lips illuminated her features, and once again she couldn't help but blush. Still she tried to play cool.

"Lots of girls come in here day after day," she said. "I'm not the only one blessed with having green eyes, you know."

"I won't argue with you on that. But I've got clues, if you still want to know."

"What clues?" she looked at him suspiciously.

"I know what you ate yesterday—I came back and enquired from the waitress who served you. You had a chicken noodle soup, a whooper, and ice cream."

She shook her head. "Those weren't what I had. What I had was—"

She paused when she realised the trick he'd made her fall into and it brought a burst of laughter from her.

"Alright, you've got me. That was me that you saw."

"The guy you were with yesterday, who was he?"

"Now why would you want to know that?"

He shrugged. "No harm, I'm just making conversation. If you don't want to answer, it's no harm."

"No harm on my part either," she said. "That was my boyfriend."

Zee nodded his head as he'd expected this. "That's nice. How come you're not here with him today?"

"Why? Is it a crime to be alone without my boyfriend beside me?"

"It's no crime, but if I were in his shoes, I wouldn't let you out the front door without posting a couple of Secret Service guys to watch your back."

"That's quite a line. Do the ladies all fall for it when you use it on them?"

"The pretty ones do. The rest just tell me to mind my own business, but you're too beautiful to use that line on me. Besides, it's an innocent type of question."

"Listening to you talk, I'll bet nothing stays innocent with you for long," she sniggered. "But if you must know, he's not here with me because he's got lots of stuff to do I guess."

"Then he's not your boyfriend," Zee declared.

Her eyes flashed at him speculatively. "Whatever makes you think that?"

"You being here and him being out there and you not knowing where he is right now or what he's doing. Chances are that he too wouldn't know about you being here or whom you're with right now. Either way, it's a good thing he's not around, or else my job would be a bit difficult."

"What sort of job is that?"

"I want to ask you out on a date," he said it with a straight face.

She laughed at the same time looked at him incredulously as if expecting a joke. "You're serious. You want to ask me out on a date, just like that."

"I can't think of any other way I'd like to put it, but yes, just like that will do."

"But I already told you I've got a boyfriend."

"That's fine with me," he said. "I'm not here stealing you from him, neither am I trying to mess up his game. I just want a date with you. Simple as that. Tell me where and when."

She kept on looking at him, marvelled by his audacity, yet taken by it. "I don't believe this. I don't even know you … or your name."

"I'm Zee," he stretched forth his hand. She shook it.

"Zee," she murmured. "Is that your name, or are you a rapper or something?"

"Actually, it's Zeke, but most people call me Zee. So how about yours?"

"Tonia."

"Nice knowing you, Tonia. So how about that date?"

"I don't know, I'm going to have to think about it. This whole thing is like a rush."

"How about I give you a call later this evening?"

They exchanged phone numbers. He glanced at his watch, saw that he needed to be on the move real soon.

"It's time for me to make my leave, Tonia," he got up and once again shook her hand. "Was really nice chatting with you. Hope we can extend it soon enough."

"I'll just have to think about it, won't I?"

"I'm sure you will. I'll be expecting your call."

He said goodbye to her and rushed out of the restaurant into the rain towards his car. He reversed his car and saw her looking at him from inside and they waved at each other as he drove off.

Got ya! Zee thought with a touch of smile on his lips.

***

Minx lived on a sloping residential area called Apple Hill with her husband of seven years, a daughter of twenty from a previous marriage, a five year old son from her present marriage, and a Cheshire cat called Spock, named after that famous character in *Star Trek*. She was one of Zee's thriving sluts and even though she was in her fifties, still she had the pussy, tits, and could fuck like a twenty year old. She loved everything about having sex, and where there were black men involved, she very much wanted to be there to party. Her husband knew about her lifestyle and loved the fact that she was getting steady supply of black cocks and bringing back home as much creampie for him to clean up.

Minx had an almost insatiable libido, something that's been with her first she lost her virginity to her neighbour's son when she was seventeen. Though she'd be the last to claim that she was a nympho. "I just love fucking, Zee," she'd explained to him one night after they'd fucked all through the evening, passing a blunt back and forth. "I love getting my pussy and ass fucked and I enjoy fucking a stiff cock in me—preferably black—but that don't make me no nympho."

Zee could have cared less what she was or wasn't. She loved to fuck and wasn't ashamed of declaring it, that was more than enough for him.

Minx had a 'BLACK COCKS ONLY' tattoo stencilled on her crotch. Her former and present husbands were the only white pricks she'd had since she discovered the joy of black cocks when back in college. Zee had never introduced her to white guys and knew she wouldn't even be impressed if she met one who packed a John Holmes-type cock in his pants. Zee was the only black stud she invited into her home to fuck, and anytime he wanted her, she was game. Her first husband couldn't keep up with her wants and had ended this amicably with her; her second, Lionel, was trying. Her daughter was well aware of her lifestyle and lots of times she had peeped in on her and Zee fucking in the master bedroom and had for months been expressing interest in wanting her mom to introduce her into the line of business. Minx had told Zee about her, and he too was aptly looking forward to taking out that young pussy of hers soon.

The downpour had just about turned into a drizzle when Zee drove into her street. He entered their stuccoed driveway and honed his horn as he came to a stop. At that moment the front door opened and out came a young girl and a young lad, both locked in conversation just as Zee got down from his car. The young girl turned from her companion and looked at his direction and almost immediately her eyes lit up with recognition. The young girl was Carmen, Minx's twenty year old daughter. She departed from the pleading features of the guy she was with and came over to hug Zee.

"Zee! Long time no see!" she wrapped her arms affectionately around him. Zee did the same thing, enjoying the feel of her budding breasts behind her tank top for a moment before pulling away from her; he saw that she'd studded her tongue.

She was a younger and beautiful version of her mother: thick brown hair, high cheek bones with a pair of perfect lips. Her lips

42

looked just ripe enough to handle a good dick, what with that perfect smile of hers, Zee thought to himself. He couldn't help checking the curve of her hips in the pair of jeans she had on as they walked away from his ride.

"Carmen, you're looking lovelier than a rose. How're you doing, girl?"

"I'm fine, thanks. We haven't seen you in a while; I thought you were out of town."

"Busy bee, that who I be. Why you think I was out of town?"

"Because I stopped by your place last Monday. You here to see Mom?"

"Oh yeah." He noticed the guy she was with standing alone with himself, looking like a love-sick puppy that's been left under the rain. He didn't ask who he was, she caught the hint.

"His name's Jerry," she whispered into his ear.

"Your boyfriend?" he whispered back the question.

"No, but wants to be." She turned towards the young man. "Hey, Jerry, come over here let me introduce you to someone."

Zee noted the way she called the young man over: such a command, much the same sort of voice her mom used on her dad when in his cuckold stance. Jerry shuffled over to meet them and she introduced him to Zee. Already a wimp in the making, Zee thought at the same time felt sorry for the young lad.

"How's it hanging, Jerry?" Zee said as he shook his hand.

"Uh … everything's fine, sir," Jerry mumbled.

"Yeah, everything looks fine already," Zee muttered.

Carmen dismissed Jerry, told him she would see him at school tomorrow. Jerry muttered goodbye to her and then took off. Zee took a last look at the kid as he went scurrying down the street and couldn't stop himself from laughing.

"That's some lad you've got there," he said to Carmen. "He seems to worship you already."

"Yes, he does. He used to follow me around in school, always trying to ask me out on a date. I keep telling him I have a boyfriend, but he says he doesn't care. You're all the boyfriend that I need. But I'm still mad at you."

"Mad at me for what?"

"You know." She held up his hand and his palm with her fore finger; Zee got the hint. "Know what I mean now?" she asked him mischievously.

"I do know what you mean. But your mom told me to keep clear until she figures you're ready. Besides that, you know where my pad is, you can drop by anytime you want."

"That's what I did last week but you weren't around. I asked mom and she told me you'd gone out of town."

"You could have given me a call. Much better than dropping by unexpected."

"I wanted to surprise you that way," she said. "I was free from school and really wanted to crash at your place."

"We can still make it happen this weekend then. You can and stay through it if you want."

"Yeah, that really would be nice. I might even bring a friend along."

The front door came open and standing there was Minx's husband, Tom. He was fifty-five years old, gut-bellied with a bald plate on his head. He moved aside or Zee to enter his home—a white slave in servitude.

"It's so good to see you again, master Zee, said Tom, brimming with happiness at his arrival.

"Good to be around, Tom. Where's the Mrs?"

"Upstairs freshening up."

Zee went past him and went up the stairs. Carmen, always so curious whenever Zee came by, followed a few steps behind. Tom returned to the living room to continue with the TV program he'd been viewing, unconcerned with whatever was bound to happen in his bedroom upstairs; if his presence was required, he knew he would be called upon.

Zee stopped at the master bedroom door and knocked on it, heard a woman's voice enquire who it was.

"Yo Minx, babe, it's your main man, Zee."

"Come right in, darling," the woman's voice called out.

Zee entered the bedroom and took in the sight of Minx lying on the bed dressed in a purple & black-lined corset and black thigh-highs with a pair of pump high heels, smiling broadly at him. Her legs stood open and her hands were wrapped around the balls of a life-sized black dildo, the head which she had fucking her cunt. Minx was an ample-sized with shoulder-length brown hair that had a lightning streak of grey on the left side of her face, and her complexion was almost that of alabaster. Always a slut who couldn't have enough dick for a day.

"Zee!" she screeched and then sat up on the bed. "I thought you weren't going to drop by."

"Why's everybody getting that idea lately?" He came over to the bed and kissed her, reaching a hand behind to cop a feel of her round bottom. "How come you're up here playing with yourself alone?"

She shrugged. "Couldn't find a handsome black man around to take care of me. None except for that tired-assed husband of mine." She threw aside her dildo and started feeling over his crotch. "I've been a bad, naughty girl all morning with nothing to place with except my dildo. I need me a black cock right now."

"I feel you, babe. It's why I came to remind you about—"

She brought a finger to his lips, cutting him off. "I don't want to hear about no other, not now, Zee. I just told you I need a black cock, and I'm so horny right now, I can hardly care about anything else you might say."

Her fingers moved so fast undoing Zee's belt and jeans button and then reaching inside to claim her prize. His cock was semierect when it came to light, but with a few deft strokes it charged itself to life. Minx smiled as she bent her head and took his cock into her mouth. She murmured a loving sigh as she sucked his cock, rolling her tongue around his shaft's helmet then swallowing him once again.

Carmen stood by the doorway peeping through the half-opened door at what her mom and Zee was engaged in. She stood in the passageway with one foot past her parent's bedroom doorway. She had one hand working her crotch while the other caressed her breasts from inside her tank top. Her breathing came in harsh gasps and when she couldn't take it anymore, pushed the door open and entered her parent's bedroom.

Zee by now had his jeans hanging halfway down his thighs and Minx came to her knees before him. His cock jutted before him like an arrow, the head buried between Minx's unforgiving lips. Carmen approached him from behind and slapped his buttocks. Neither Zee nor Minx appeared surprised to see her standing there. Minx looked up from her sucking and smiled at her, glad today would be the day her daughter took her first step towards being fucked by a real cock. Zee kissed Carmen then lowered his head to wrap his lips around one of her perky tits. His other hand dove into her open jeans to finger the sensitive skin hiding behind her panties. His finger slipped between her cunt lips and Carmen held him tight and gave a moaning cry as he started finger-fucking her. She nibbled on his ear lobe, grinding and pushing her hips forward to the pull of Zee's fingers. Her moans got to a crescendo when Zee inserted two fingers into her cunt at the same time rubbed his thumb against her clit, spurring her into cumming so suddenly. She fell to the bed, gasping. Mink stopped to laugh at her before continuing with Zee's cock in her mouth. Carmen freed herself from her clothes and came to kneel beside her mom. Minx glanced at her daughter and saw the light burning in her eyes.

"Mom, may I …"

She needn't say anymore. "Sure, honey." Minx took her mouth from Zee's shaft and offered it to her daughter.

Carmen stroked his cock and applied her mouth to it tentatively, as if expecting it to bite at her. Minx caressed her daughter's hair at the same time watched as she engulfed her mouth over Pimp Zee's prick. Carmen immersed herself, wanting to impress Zee and her mom with her actions. She flicked the tip of her studded tongue around the piss slit before forcing her mouth to take his shaft. A moment later Minx took his cock from her and Zee watched as mother and daughter passed his cock back and forth to each other like a Frisbee. Minx and Carmen took turns sucking on his cock and attending to his balls; sometimes their tongue met with his shaft between their lips. Zee held their head and told them to go ahead and kiss each other. Mother and daughter locked lips with each other; Zee caressed their hair while they did so, totally loving the sight.

They led Zee to the bed.

Mom and daughter helped him out of his clothes; their hands kept brushing against his cock. Minx indicated her daughter to sit over Zee's face. While Carmen leaned forward and resumed sucking his cock, Minx came from behind to eat her pussy along with Zee. She spread her daughter's ass cheeks aside and Zee pulled at her fleshy cunt lips while Minx kissed her daughter's unblemished ass cheek before dipping her tongue into her puckered anal hole. Zee dug deep under Carmen's weight and twirled and pushed his tongue further into her pussy, sucking in her cum while her mother finger-fucked her ass; sometimes she and Zee shared a kiss before once again concentrating on Carmen's cunt. Carmen's body couldn't stop responding to what they were doing to her. She whimpered and shook from the double pleasure she was getting. She returned her mouth to the bulbous head of Zee's cock; her moans became muffled gasps. Zee still had his lips locked on the young girl's pussy and he held onto her waistline as he felt himself unleash his torrent of cum straight inside her mouth. Carmen was unprepared for it and nearly choked on his cum as suddenly she felt it smack against the tip of her throat. She was gagging on it and coughed out a thick load which poured down Zee's thighs; Minx appeared before her and helped lick the spilled cum from Zee's thighs.

"Don't fight it, darling," Minx cautioned her daughter as she finished ingesting the spilled cum. Carmen watched her mouth and applied herself to what she was doing. "Don't be scared of it, dear. Cum is good for you, especially a black man's cum. Never let it spill or go to waste. Swallow it, go ahead; even your dad does it good."

Carmen did as her mom advised and licked off more and more of Zee's cum. She took his cock back into her mouth and sucked on it. Minx licked off the bits of cum on her cheeks and when finished, mother and daughter shared a passionate kiss and they both laughed at what they'd just achieved. Carmen rolled off Zee and he admired both women.

"That's going to be the first and last time you get to spill my cum, Carmen," he said to her.

"I promise never to do it again," she complied.

"I know you won't. Minx, your daughter's really going places, you know that, don't you?"

"Oh yeah," Minx smiled with motherly pride. "She's a slut in the making. Every time peeping through my bedroom door whenever we're in here, always asking me to beg you to pimp her out. You think you can open up a spot for her?"

"Oh most definitely." His hand went to stroking his shaft back to life. "Though we're going to have to test that pussy out first. Gotta test-drive it right about now, know what I mean."

"Oh yeah, I can't wait," Carmen answered with glee.

It was now Minx's turn to straddle Zee's face. She crossed her leg legs over him and wiggled her buttocks over his face. Within seconds Zee's tongue was sliding up and down her wet entrance and she moaned from it. Carmen sucked on Zee's cock for a while, getting it hard once again, then her mom indicated for her to climb on top of it. Carmen did just that, guiding the head of his cock under her pussy and letting it slip inside her. Minx held her daughter and caressed her tits as she gently began to ride the black cock she was resting on. Carmen pushed down her mom's corset and leaned forward to suck on her tits. But the thrill of Zee's cock filling her pussy was too much excitement for her to contain.

"Yeeeoooooowww ... Aaahhhhh ..." Carmen screamed and her eyes flew wide open and her hips took on a power of their own and began propelling her up and down on Zee's thighs. Each time her ass cheeks seemed to slam down heavy on him, stifling her breath as she felt his cock press further inside her. Her mom pulled her forward and now was nibbling on her tits. It was too much for Carmen to take; she felt herself cumming almost right away. Her cry was sharp and piercing when it happened.

"OHHHH ...SHIT! OHHH FUCK!"

She wanted to fall off him but Zee's hands grasped her waistline and held her tight. He was now pumping his cock harder against her slamming buttocks, sending more and more hurting delight into her womb. Carmen struggled to fight back, grounding her ass down on him, except each time he slammed back at her she felt her air supply cut off. Minx came off Zee's face and sat back and rubbed her pussy while she watched her daughter and her pimp/ lover fuck. She picked up her black dildo and went on fucking her cunt with it, at the same time fingering her asshole.

Carmen got over her orgasmic delight and started rocking her ass back and forth over Zee's dick; her face a mask of pain and hurt and delight rolled into one. He pulled her down towards him, their lips brushed each other's and they kissed hungrily. He spread his legs and grasping her ass cheeks and went on pounding her pussy from underneath. Carmen's features tightened like she was really hurting and she wouldn't stop screaming all the while he sank his cock in and out of her. He turned her over and brought her legs over his shoulder and resumed ramming his cock harder and harder into her pussy. Zee was breathing hard against her face. Carmen gazed down at the sight of his back dick driving deep between her legs, looking like he wanted to split her open. She wouldn't stop howling as he fucked her more and more into submission.

"Oh my God! Oh my God! Ohh Shit!" she cried so loud her feet came down Zee's shoulder and locked themselves behind his thighs. Still it didn't slow him down from fucking her.

"You like that, bitch?" Zee gasped. "You like how my dick's fucking you, right?"

"Uhhh … yeah!" she cried amidst her moans. "Ohhh yeah … I do … *I FUCKING DO!*"

Minx came behind Zee and rimmed his ass while he went on fucking her daughter. She lay on her back and tugged on his balls. Zee pulled out of Carmen for a moment and allowed Minx to clean his cock before slipping it back into her daughter's awaiting cunt and resumed fucking it. How she wished she were nineteen all over again, Minx thought as she withdrew and went back to fucking her dildo. Then she would have all the black cocks she could afford and never end up getting hitched to a cuck wimp like her husband downstairs.

She watched as Zee struggled to pull himself up from the bed, pulling her daughter along. Carmen tightened her grip around him and though they at first stumbled, he managed to pull her up to his feet. His cock fell out of her. Minx came and sucked on it then returned it back inside her. Carmen began screaming once again as Zee went on hammering his cock against her fuck hole. Their thighs slapped against each other. Her cries reverberated around the room, falling in rhythm with the pounding she was receiving.

"Ohhh Shit! Oh my God! I'm gonna cum-I'm gonna cum-*I'M GONNA CUMMMM!*"

She shrieked while still grasping a-hold of Zee's sweaty shoulders. When he was done, he dropped her down on the bed and left her gasping. He grabbed Minx by the head and pulled her forward to suck on his tool. Carmen lay there trembling for the bout of fucking she'd just received, wondering if she was still alive or was already in Heaven. She could still feel Zee's cock in her, even though he wasn't fucking her anymore. She watched her mom suck on his cock and then he made her be on all fours and entered her cunt from behind. He took Minx like she was his, like she was nothing but a fuck tool. His back muscles glistened with sweat. Minx groaned nonstop from the might of her lover's cock drilling her cunt.

Zee turned to Carmen when he saw she's gotten some strength back and said, "Bring yourself over here, girl!"

She came dutifully, kneeling beside his feet. Her eyes marvelled at the sight of his cock pushing back and forth into her mother's wide cunt.

"Come over her," Zee indicated where he wanted her to be. "Widen you mom's ass for me."

Carmen stood above her mother and grasped her ass cheeks and held them apart as Zee told her to. He pulled out of her mom's pussy, offered it to her to suck clean, and then pressed its bulbous head into Minx's asshole. Minx grasped the bed sheets and yelped from the hurting pain of his cock pushed through. The pain was immense, but she knew it would soon go away. She smiled and wiggled her butt to take in his cock further.

"Oh yeah, fuck me, Zee!" she shouted. "Go on, fuck my ass!"

Zee grunted and spat down on her anal hole as he went on fucking it. He smacked her butt repeatedly each time he pulled out of her. Carmen grasped her Mom's ass and urged Pimp Zee to keep fucking her: "Yeah, Zee. Go on fuck her! Fuck Mom's ass real good!"

Zee gritted his teeth, groaning from the incredible tightness that gripped his shaft. He quickened the pace of his fucking until the moment when he couldn't hold it back anymore.

"Aww shit!" he groaned. "*AWW FUCKING SLUT! FUCK! GADDAMN!*"

He pulled his cock at the exact moment and began jerking furiously. Minx fell flat on the bed, totally spent. Carmen came forward, following the sight of Zee's cock and opened her mouth to him. Zee couldn't stop groaning as he pumped his load successively, shooting each spurt into her gaping mouth. She took in every drop, including the ones that poured out the side of her mouth. When he was done, Zee fell to the bed soon was joined by mom and daughter lying on either side of him, caressing his torso.

He turned to Minx and said: "Next time, I'll cum inside ... then we'll get your old man to clean up."

Minx laughed. "I'm surprised you haven't thought of that yet."

Carmen raised her head. "Does this mean you're going to pimp me as well?" she asked.

"Girl," Zee said. "You're it already. Hope you've got a good pair of high heels and some thong panties, 'cause you and your mama are getting hit today."

***

Zee, out of sheer necessity, always kept a small bag of clothes in his women's homes in case he needed a quick change-over, knowing that they almost always looked forward to him spending the night. He showered and changed into a sports tee shirt of his and went downstairs to sit with Minx's husband while both women hurried about getting themselves in order for the outing he'd planned. He made idle chat with Tom as they watched a football game on the TV, while Spock slinked its tail around his ankle.

The women joined them downstairs nearly an hour later, both of them looking gorgeous and lovely in a pair of evening outfit.

They both had on a pair of high heels, and as they stood beside each other, letting husband/father and pimp/lover admire them, it was hard to presume that they were mother and daughter.

Tom escorted his wife and daughter to Zee's jeep and he shared a kiss with both women before they got into his car and drove off. When seeing the car's tail lights disappear from down the street, Tom rushed back inside the house, went upstairs to dig out his hidden stash of porn movies. He had been wanting to masturbate so bad all the time Zee had been fucking both women; it was too bad they hadn't called him upstairs to come and watch.

Zee arrived at the exotic-looking house where the supposed party was taking place and drove into the courtyard where a fleet of hot looking rides were parked. Loud music was blaring, and the place was filled with party revellers. He parked his jeep near the gate's entrance and he walked both women into the mansion to introduce them to the host. He gave mother and daughter a kiss and promised to see them later before leaving them in the care of the host who already was feeling his hand up Carmen's skirt.

It was almost dusk when he drove back to his condo. He felt like he could close his eyes and doze off and never think of coming awake for the next two days. He wasn't complaining though. Plenty of days were just like this, and with his steady growth of women and clients on the rise, he'd long made himself gotten used to it.

He let himself into his pad and went into the bathroom to have a shower. An hour later he'd fixed himself an evening meal and just then he thought about Tonia, the pretty brunette at MacDonald's. He picked up his phone and scrolled through her number and pressed the dial button.

"I can always wait tomorrow," he muttered to himself. "Tomorrow for sure."

He washed his plate then went and laid his head on the bed. His phone rang while he slept but he never came awake to pick it up. That night, he slept like the dead.

Three Days in Charleston

Day 1
Monday, 27th August 2012

Washington National Airport (DCA)—
Charleston International Airport (CHS)

05:40p.m – 07:14p.m.

He got delayed leaving Ronald Reagan National airport. That was to be expected; he had an additional thirty minutes to wait. The white couple down in Charleston, S.C., we're expecting him. He gave them a call and sent the wife an erotic text message saying he'd be with her soon. Only a matter of time.

He sat in the lounge area, took a novel out of his knapsack bag and read while his eyes periodically checked the time on his watch to make sure he wasn't going to miss his flight; the time on his wristwatch was still tuned one hour ahead of Greenwich/ Nigerian time. He always thought of home whenever he was alone. His eyes scanned the people walking past him in the airport. He never failed to notice especially the women. In his mind he played a little game where he assigned them a history. Whether he was right or wrong didn't bother him, it was his game after all.

Here came this tall, lanky blonde. Thin jaw line in black skirt and blouse pulling a bag behind her. Looked like a secretary. Looked somewhat stuck-up … But who knows. Who really knows what a freak she just might be. Some women, he knew this for a fact, kept things hidden even when they're married. Most keep it that way while at the same time waiting and hoping for the right man to come along. The right man who's got the right code to get right to the point and get her fuck urges rocking. A lot of hubbies out there get hitched to a docile woman and don't even realize that with the right type of brother, that housewife would turn into a randy bitch with no damn care at all. Another thing he knew is this is something a lot of husbands out there want of their women but most are too scared to ask. Wimps, is what he called such men.

He sat there and for his personal amusement tried to picture the sex life of some of the couples who came and went past him. There were college kids in shorts and halter tops chatting on their phones or to their friends, there were alone women who sat down with a book in hand or a tablet, there were mothers playing with their kids and others there with their men beside them. He tried to imagine what the women would be like in bed with their men … but also what they would be like in bed with him.

There came the announcement and he had time to send the South Carolina couple a last text message letting them know he was about boarding his flight before heading towards the checkout gate. He buckled himself into his seat and glanced out the aisle window at the sight that was an cool evening in Washington D.C. Minutes later his plane ran down the runway and roared into the sky.

The journey lasted two hours; it felt like forty minutes. The sky was deep purple when his flight came back down to earth and taxied down the runway towards it's off-loading spot and the pilot came on the mike and on behalf of US Airways welcomed him and the other passengers to Charleston, South Carolina. He got his bag out the overhead compartment and joined the crowd stepping out the belly of the plane and into the airport.

The wife's hubby was waiting for him as he left the baggage-claim area and they shook hands. He hubby—Adam, his name is— welcomed him to Charleston and helped him with his knapsack as they strolled into the airport's lounge area which was starting to close down. His wife, Sally, was waiting for both of them there. She wore a knee-length purple dress and white stockings; inside the car he would discover she wore nothing underneath. She hugged him. They shared a kiss—"Welcome, darling," she said to him. They took a snapshot together in the airport lounge before leaving the building.

Their car was waiting in the parking lot—a discreet-looking van. He and the wife slid into the backseat with her skirt riding up her thigh and giving him an eye-full of her nakedness underneath—which was how he'd told her two days back to be dressed for him—while her husband went into the front and started the car and then drove out of the airport's parking lot.

The car had tinted windows so no one outside could see what was happening inside. Though he would much have preferred that others saw what was happening. Shango enjoyed being risky and adventurous sometimes. It got his blood pumping when attempting something he ought not to, especially in places few would dare.

He pulled the wife into his arms and they immediately kissed. The kiss was strong and passionate, the sort lovers would give when having being away from each other for so long a time. She slid her tongue in and out of his mouth and he too did the same to her. He reached for her thigh and pushed it upwards and felt her naked flesh underneath and realized she was wet and anxious for him and wouldn't stop moaning as he rubbed his thumb and index finger over the warm surface that was her labia. She twitched in his arms like she'd been goosed. She groaned persistently as they kissed, pressing herself into his arms, giving herself totally to him. She moaned and whispered how much she'd been longing to have him; he muttered the same to her.

Their hands groped and held and caressed each other as their thighs rubbed together. She straddled him; her breathing frantic. He folded her purple dress in his hand and slapped her fleshy bottom; she groaned from it. His cock pressed against the top of his jeans wanting to be let loose. He made her lie on the backseat and came down from it, holding her legs wide apart. His only source of light in the car were the street lights with their fluorescent bulbs they passed along the way. He sank his lips on her pussy and she arched herself and cried so loud, at the same time pressed his head downward as his tongue invaded and probed her treasure zone. Her body shook all over. He hummed to himself as his tongue found her clitoris and flicked it like he would a light switch. She shrieked and squirted over his face. He didn't pull away; he lapped up her love juice and poured some of it down into her cunt and licked it back up again. Her husband checked on them repeated as he drove, asking if they were having any fun; the wife could barely reply as she was panting like one out of breath. Still she kept on screaming inside the confines of the car and still squirting as he sucked on her pussy.

They got to a red light and then he stopped and sat on the chair while she remained on her back catching her breath. She murmured to herself as she fought down her moans to get her voice back, laughing and amazed at what he'd done to her in so little a time. She wanted to repay the favour. She came to him and undid his belt buckle and pushed his jeans down his thigh and jockey shorts and freed his cock out. By now her dress had fallen down to her waistline and her hair looked a mess but she didn't care. She blew on his cock and then sucked on the helmet tip before slipping her mouth down to take more of him. She murmured to him between breaks as she sucked his prick.

'—such a lovely black cock …'

Mmmmmm …

'—wanting your black master cock for so long …'

Mmmmmmm …

'—going to tell my friends about you … Mmmmm … Make them jealous too …'

Her head bobbed up and down between his legs. Her lips made slurping sounds as if she was munching on an ice cream. The red light turned green and her husband drove on. He switched on the front interior lights and got a good view of his wife concentrating on pleasing her Black Master while she fingered her pussy.

They made a stop at a restaurant to get her lover something to eat as it had been a long journey for him. Sally wore back her dress and tied her thick brunette hair in a knot while he returned his black prick behind his shorts and zipped back his jeans. Adam waited for them to finished dressing before they stepped out of the car and crossed the wide parking space towards the restaurant. The husband led the way while the wife and her lover held hands and followed.

Such was how Master Shango spent his first two hours in Charleston.

***

It had been a long day and it was going to get even longer for the three of them.

Black Master Shango was hungry and he hadn't realized how much he was until they entered the restaurant. His eyes sized up the place and loved the look and feel of it. They were given a table and he and Sally sat next to each other while the husband picked up the menu booklet and ordered for the three of them; Shango ordered for a beer—Bud Lite.

They made conversation while they waited for their meal to arrive. Adam enquired about the trip. They talked about the impending hurricane happening down in Louisiana and how its fall-out was going to give them a dull weather all through this week. Sally wouldn't stop rubbing her hand over his thigh. Her breathing was still heavy from the bout of excitement she'd had in the car—obviously she hadn't been expecting such, and she did eventually say it. It made Shango's heart swell to hear and feel her response. He most enjoyed it when a woman becomes relaxed around him. He wasn't a practical lover as most black men would claim to be online. Sally reckoned such was something he'd obviously written down as to how or what he was going to come at her with, but she couldn't have been farther from the truth. And she was bound to realize that during their period together.

Their meal arrived and they ate. Sally still rubbed her hand across his thigh and he too ran his over her inner thigh, even slipped his finger into her cunt and brought it to his lips. He loved the way she tasted; he couldn't wait to taste more of her when alone.

The young man who had served them—he claimed he was from Canada originally—asked if everything was to our satisfaction, which we replied that it was. Sally opened to him about her lover:

"You're in the presence of a writer who's soon to become famous," she said with delight. "Have you read that 'Fifty Shades' book? He writes just like that, except I enjoy his because it's ten-times more erotic. His name is Shango, and you can find him at blackmastershango.com. Tell everyone in here about him."

Shango was caressing her thigh and smiling at her while she said it. The Canadian waiter did take notice of where his hand was and he didn't care, neither did Sally or Adam. He wrote down the site's address on his notebook and bid the three of them goodnight we they got up from their table to leave. He was probably going to have a lot of fun when he mentioned about them to the other female staff inside the restaurant, if ever he did.

They returned to the car—Adam in the driver's seat while Shango and Sally returned to the back. Now he had some strength in him, he got back to what he had been doing earlier. He had his arm over the back of her neck and caressed her left breasts while he kissed her and then applied his lips to her other, flipping his tongue over the pair of gold stud she had on her nipples. Her body pressed against his; her legs crossed over his and rubbed against his thigh. She moaned and panted like a wild cat. The pool of light from the street lamps gave them both an erotic outlook of themselves in each other's arms.

His finger dove into her pussy and he finger-fucked her while his mouth held hers and listened to her groaning voice as she couldn't stop screaming. Her hand gripped his and now her legs pressed together his hand which now as locked between her thigh. Still she gasped and groaned into his mouth. She had never been this loose before with another man … and yes, there have been other men before him, but with Shango, she felt a rapid stirring deep in her bowels she'd never had before. Her was driving her insane, making her succumb to all perversity that had always evaded her.

He pulled his hand out of her cunt and gave her his finger to clean up, which she did, still panting. He returned the finger into her cunt, heard her striving to control her screams but whispered into her ear to let it out … he wanted to hear her scream … which she did. Her pussy wouldn't stop leaking her cum juice. He made her lie on her backside and he licked his tongue up and down her cunt. He felt her squirt a river down her legs. Her body spasmed like she was being electrocuted.

He undid his belt buckle and pushed his jeans and shorts down his legs and brought her to climb on top of him; he would have loved her to sit over his face had the car being any higher. Sally straddled him, groaning into his ear as he reached his hand underneath to find her pussy opening. It was easy as she was still leaking like an open faucet.

"Awwhhhh God, I want your cock so bad," she moaned into his ear, kissing the side of his neck. "I want you … I want you so much!"

"I want you too," he replied back and kissed her.

He slid the head of his prick into her pussy and she cried out helplessly at the same time bucked her body against him as she felt his dick inside her for the first time. The car went over a speed bump. His cock went inside her all the way and now she rode him with her tits slapping against his face and she crying from the ecstatic pain she was in. Her hair went loose and fell over her head. His hands slapped her ass cheeks, making her yearn for more. She wouldn't stop screaming and he kept urging her to scream more. He too groaned against her. The feel and tightness of her pussy was the greatest thing he could think about at that moment.

"Aahhhh! Aaaahhhh!"

Her cries pierced the confines of the vehicle. She kept grounding herself against him. Her body grew taut with desire. She climaxed over and over again. He could feel her body tremble. She pumped harder and continued to ride him. Numerous times his cock slipped out of her pussy, her juice now stained his thighs and poured down the car seat to wet his legs. Frantic, she reached for his cock and tucked it back inside her.

She came off him after climaxing again. She sprawled on the seat and he now came on top of her and resumed fucking her again. Her pussy was so moist it took a couple seconds for his cock to remain still inside her. His dick made a squishing sound each time he drove it in her. It was too bad there wasn't enough leg room inside the vehicle. Still he kept on fucking her harder and harder … till his own moment arrived and he felt himself let loose his spunk inside her.

They sat up on the backseat, hugging each other, both gasping for breath … and laughing too.

"Welcome to Charleston, Master Shango," she said to him.

"Why thank you, Sally."

They both laughed; Adam too joined them.

The vehicle left the main road and took a side street into a quiet residential neighbourhood. Everybody was long tucked inside; their nearest neighbour lived a quarter of a mile from them. Adam drove into their yard and came to a stop in front of a garage. A hairy cat was there to welcome them. Sally and Shango wore back their clothes and he helped her with her shoes before they stepped out of the car and walked into the house, pushing open a screen door and letting the cat inside.

It began to rain some minutes later.

Theirs was a big house and a very quiet one too with just the two of them and the cat—the kids have all grown and left. They have the freedom to be themselves however they want. According to Adam, aside from work, they had little or nothing else to do.

Shango and Sally had the large bedroom to themselves, most especially the king-sized bed. He stowed his bag in the closet and she joined him in the bathroom and they showered with together. He wanted to save her for later in the night, but her body responded differently. They scrubbed each other's body, and he placed her leg on a stand and eat her pussy while water from the shower rained down on them. Adam told them goodnight before retiring upstairs.

The sex continued from where they'd left off in the car after they'd dried themselves and climbed into bed and switched off the light. Sally slid closer to him under the covers, loved the feel of his arms around her. Her hand stroked his cock and she would stop giggling and kissing him. He commented that she looked so young and beautiful as she was … like a college girl. They pushed themselves out the bed covers and she reclined downward to suck his cock while he pushed her hair off from her face. He turned on a bedside lamp to see her clearly. Her hands felt cold when she caressed his balls. He forced her head down on his dick, loved the look on her face with her mouth wrapped around his meat. He told her she made him feel so good. His cock was so erect he felt like it would break off his crotch.

Sally came on top of him, reached underneath to guide his cock into her pussy. Her pussy felt tight, but it didn't take long for him to rub her clit and she groaned from it that her wetness lubricated her entrance and his cock slipped into her with little resistance. She grind against him; her lips hollered and she was screaming again. So loud it would have woken the neighbours if any was there to hear them … and Shango would have loved that to happen as well. He kept slapping her ass, pumping his thighs and thrusting more of his cock into her. She leaned backward and caressed his balls while still grinding her hips against him. Her hands went to her head and pulled at her hair; she shrieked almost endlessly.

"Awwhhhnnnn God! Aahhhhwwwnnn God! I want you … I want your black cock!"

He pulled her face towards his, groaning back at her.

"You want that black cock, don't you?"

"Ohhh yes! I want it! I want your fucking black cock to fuck me! *FUCK ME!*"

He pulled his cock out of her and sprayed the back of her ass with his semen. Still he remained hard. He slipped his prick back inside her pussy and kept pounding her again. The bed responded to their weight. He fingered her asshole. He lost count of her climax and wouldn't have cared. He bit on her breasts, rubbed his teeth against her nipples. He felt his erection dying inside her. She collapsed beside him, kissing his lips and face, murmuring to him how happy she was to have him in her bed.

"I love you, Master Shango," she said.

The rain continued to fall outside.

***

Sally couldn't get enough of Master Shango.

She was overwhelmed with so much excitement it was hard for her to contain the rapture she was feeling. All the weeks and months of communicating with him, the hours they'd spent talking to each other on the phone, listening to the sound of his voice coming from miles away. Her falling in love with his voice and all the while picturing what he might look like when standing in front of her. Night after night she'd ached and worried over him and about him. How often she and Adam had conversed about what better way to receive him … what sort of man he would be … but mostly, if he was genuine and hopping he would be everything they both dreamed and hopped he would be. Everything right there and then of having him in her bedroom just seemed to eclipse right there and then as she and Adam introduced him into her home, and then now that she laid in bed under the sheets beside him, naked. They'd just finished making love but still she wasn't ready to go to sleep. In any case, sleep didn't seem to want to come to her; she was too much in her excitement to want that to happen.

"I can't tell you how much I've wanted to meet with you," she said to him.

She drew close to him there was no space between them except for the thick bed covers they laid under. Her legs came under his. Her hands wouldn't stop feeling over his face, caressing the thin growth of hair that formed his beard. Her hand left his face and rubbed his shoulder and arm muscles while his ran over her backside, over her rump, and then came forward and tweaked her nipples; she hissed every time he did such, her body quivered. Her body was charged with so much electricity she was like an engine that wouldn't cool down.

"I told you I was real," he said to her.

"That was my mistake. I'm a believer now," she said.

How she loved the sound of his voice. Hearing it on the phone never ceased to get her wet. And now he was up-close with her, she could feel her wetness squelching between her labia. She wanted this man so much she couldn't think of wanting anything else.

"You worried too much," he smiled at her.

"Forgive me for that. I just never realized how … how good you would be."

"You thought I was playing."

"No, no, darling, I never thought so. It's just that … well, sometimes it's hard knowing someone who's real. Especially someone who's far from where you are."

"You were kind of hesitant about that the last time we spoke on the phone," he said. "Especially when you sent me that old posting of mine you found online."

She laughed, clearly embarrassed. "I didn't mean it. Adam and I were just fooling around when we stumbled upon it. It said that you were married. I just wanted to know if it was you or not."

"It wasn't me. I've never been married or even engaged to be."

"I know that now, darling," she wrapped her hands on his face and pressed her lips against his. "Please forgive me."

"There's nothing to forgive; it never happened."

That made her smile. "Did I tell you I always love the sound of your voice?"

"Something tells me you love my lips, too."

"Yes, I love your lips. You have the most amazing lips."

Shango pushed the sheets off their body and began kissing her breasts. Sally fell on her backside and cooed. Goosebumps broke over her arms and his lips ran over her tits and around her neck region. She raised herself up from the bed and grabbed at his head. She licked at his ears and then shot her head back over her pillow, her body taut and she let loose a shaking cry as he slipped his finger in and out of her cunt. His finger rubbed against her clit and that sent a shockwave over her body. Her pussy juice poured out of her cunt freely like a faucet being left to run, and she wouldn't stop beating her hands on the bed, screeching from what he was doing to her.

He fed on one of her tits and pulled at it at the same time flicked his tongue over her studded nipple while at the same time keeping concentration on what his finger was doing to her pussy.

At that moment the bedroom light came on. Sally looked up from the bed and Shango did too.

Her husband Adam stood by the doorway wearing a grey tee shirt and boxer shorts and flip-flops. He'd heard his wife screaming from the bedroom upstairs which used to belong to one of his sons who'd now left for college and he had temporarily converted into his own room for the duration of Master Shango's stay. He too couldn't sleep and had laid in bed imagining what Shango and his wife might be up to. Hearing his wife scream out he could tell it was they were up to something. He'd missed much of what they'd done inside the car while he drove, he didn't want to miss seeing any of their actions tonight. With that in mind, he'd left his bed and came down to watch them.

Sally knew what had brought her husband downstairs and couldn't help but laugh at the sight of her husband cradling his penis in his hand while he stood there watching them. Shango didn't say anything; he went back to the work at hand.

He held Sally's legs apart and eat her pussy; she was moaning even before he began. His licked his tongue up and down Sally's pussy and she kept pressing her hips into this face. She squirted into his face and still he eat her pussy like it was his own. Her hubby came closer to the bed to see more of what was happening. He saw his wife squirming and screaming out loud on the bed, thrashing her legs back and forth. She was struggling from Shango's grasp and yet she couldn't move. She turned to look at her husband, her face flush with hurting excitement. He came to her and held her hand, asked if she was doing alright. She tried to speak but her words came out in mumbling grunts. Her abdomen kept heaving up from the bed. She grabbed his tee shirt and with such strength pulled him down towards her as she braced herself for a shattering scream. Her pelvis went up and down her lover's face; her pussy begged for more.

"Ohhh … Awwhhh God … Oh my God! Please … make him stop! He's killing me, babe! Ohhh God, I can't … I can't cum anymore!"

She panted on her husband's shoulder. He hugged her face to his chest and kissed her forehead. He caressed one of her tits and that made his wife moan into his shirt.

Shango stood up from between her legs and wiped her cum off his lips. He came forward to her and she grabbed his face and kissed him with all passion she could muster. Her legs locked him in a vice and pulled him to her. His prick found her pussy's entrance and she inhaled as he slammed down into her.

Adam stood back and watched. His wife wasn't his anymore; Master Shango had firm hold of her now.

"Gimme your dick!" she screamed in the confines of the room. "Awwhh God! Gimme all your black dick!"

Her held him with one arm and slapped his buttocks as he ground his hips between her open legs. Her husband held one of her legs open for him. He admired the sight of Shango's shaft sinking in and out of his wife's cunt; in his mind he imagined how wide he was going to make her pussy feel by the time he returned to D.C.

Every muscle on his thighs worked as he pumped more and more of his prick into Sally's cunt. He sat up from the bed, his hands behind her head, pulling her up from where she lay, grinding her ass back and forth and panting feverishly. Adam watched the sight of his wife's round ass grinding on top of her lover's hips, listened to her screaming for him to fuck her hard. He watched as Master Shango grasped her ass cheeks and kept pushing her against him, both of them grunting in each other's face as they sought to kiss.

Shango fell on his back taking her along. Sally slapped her hands on his chest, she groaned and threw her head side to side, scattering her hair in a whirl as her body kept on obeying her lust. Her pussy was drenched in her cum. She wouldn't stop whimpering and her hips kept on riding her lover's cock, wanting him to cum so much. She could feel herself reaching the precipice once more.

His hands slapped at her butt cheeks, making her ride him harder.

"You loving that black dick, babe?"

"Uhhggghhh ... I'm loving it! I love your black dick so fucking much!"

Hot, sensations shot through her heart swirling downward in her loins. She held her breath as she felt blinding light erupting before her eyes. Her Master quickened his thrusts, getting closer to his goal. She came down on him; her hair covered his face.

"You want me to cum in you?" he breathed into her ear.

"Cum ... cum ... Agghhhhhh!"

She screamed so loud as she felt him shoot his load inside her. She fell on top of him, her pussy felt like it had been lit with gasoline. She'd never been this weakened or felt so taken by a man before; neither of her former swinging partners had ever equalled to what she just felt.

Adam went and fetched a towel from the bathroom and came and pushed her hair off her face and cleaned her features. She was still attempting to catch her breath.

"How do you feel, honey?" he asked.

She gave a weak laugh. "I dunno ... I just ... he just took me around the world. Ohh, it felt so good!"

Day 2
Tuesday 28th August 2012.

Morning came and Adam got dressed as he was off to work. He came back downstairs and checked on his wife and her lover and wasn't surprised that they were both still in bed. With the round of fucking they'd had last night, they needed the rest.

"Okay, I'll see you guys later," he waved at them.

"Okay, honey. Have a good day at work," his wife said to him.

"Yeah, holler at you later, white boi," said Shango.

Adam left the house and went out into the driveway, got into his car and drove off. In his mind he relieved all what he had seen happen in his master bedroom and got a stirring in his pants. He wouldn't be surprised they were going to fuck again as he left the house.

Later he discovered he was right after all. They did fuck again.

*****

They had the house to themselves now.

They were still in bed, neither in a hurry to get up. The bed sheets lay scattered around their feet. Sally needed to get some sleep and told Master Shango if he could allow her an hour or two to be with herself. He told her no problem. He left her in bed and went into the bathroom to shower. He came out and searched inside his bag and rubbed some lotion on his body and wore a pair of shorts. Outside the sky was overcast; it seemed it would rain any minute. He went and got his laptop and power cord out his bag and decided to roam the house.

Shango went up the stairs to one of the spare bedrooms there. He set his laptop on a library desk and connected the power cord to a socket and booted up his system. There was a window next to where he sat on a revolving chair and he could make out a driveway at the side of the house. Further out, clumps of trees blocked the view of the river. He turned on his system's Wi-Fi and checked through his emails.

There were a couple of emails waiting for him and lots of junk. Some from various hubbies across the country wanting to know more about him and how beneficial his sexual prowess can be to them; it would take him all day to respond to their mails, and once they were apt to reply back in no time once receive his replies. He checked his blog as well to know how many hits he was getting.

He was in the middle of replying one of his emails when he heard a sound coming from outside the room. He hadn't shut the door and he heard Sally calling out his name. He yelled back to let her know what room he was in. She stuck her head inside the room and entered when she saw him seated there smiling, wearing just her negligee with one arm nearly off from her shoulders.

"Hi there," she said, giggling as she came to where he sat. "I couldn't sleep. I've got you running in my head so damn much. I don't know what sort of poison you've given me, but I can't stop not wanting you."

She came and sat on his lap, pleating him with kisses. He turned his chair around, caressing her ass cheeks while she sucked on his lips, moaning as his fingers rubbed the underside of her pussy.

"Ohh God … I love it when you do that to me. Awwhhh God, Master, you drive me crazy!" She looked past his shoulder at his blog site. "Are you going to post pictures of me in there?"

"I'm thinking about it," he answered. "I'd love for couples out there to know about my time with you. But I'm going to need your permission first if you're alright with it."

"I'm very much okay with it," she breathed into his ear, rubbing the back of his neck. "But right now, I want Master Shango's cock fucking me!"

He lifted her from the chair and carried her to the bed. She held her legs for him and was already moaning aloud as he fingered her cunt then nibbled on her clit. Her cum poured out of her pussy like a dam bursting and her body couldn't stop wracking from the excitement that was on her. He came to her side of the bed and she stroked his cock and into her mouth it went. He ordered her to open her mouth wide enough to receive him.

"Yes, that's how I want you to suck me," he told her, watching her blow him. "Don't forget to suck on my balls, too."

He reached over and slipped his fingers into her cunt then bent forward to eat her pussy while she remained under him choking on his dick. His hands wrapped under her thigh and he pulled her ass up and buried his nose into her crotch. Sally jerked her hips towards his face; she made muffled groans in her mouth as she kept sucking his cock.

Outside it was splattering with rain showers; the sound of thunder exploding in the sky echoed in the room.

Shango took Sally's arm and pulled her off from the bed and brought her to where the window was and made her lean forward against it. Sally pushed down the arms of her negligee and was moaning even as her face and tits pressed against the framework of the window. Shango bent down behind her, pushed her ass cheeks aside and buried his face between her ass crack, fingering her pussy as well. Her legs shook. She pushed her ass cheeks as far backward that she could into his face; she couldn't wait for him to stick his cock into her.

He came up to his feet and made her bend forward while he searched for her pussy's entrance with his prick. She reached down between her legs to assist, rubbing it against her pussy folds before forcing it home.

"I don't care whoever's passing below," he groaned into her ear as he forced more of his dick inside her. "I want them to see … what a sexy slut you are to me."

Sally moaned with approval. She gasped from the force of his prick thrusting inside her. It was hurting, at the same time felt very nice inside her and she wanted more of it. She pushed her ass back at him. He pulled back a bit so she could bend further and now he had control of her, grabbing her waistline and thrusting harder into her. Sally groaned from the feeling. Her heart was giving her an frantic beat. She'd never been handled like this before; it felt so good and exhilarating. She looked out the window wondering if anyone was passing by; she hopped someone would.

She wished Adam was here to watch her being fucked by her Master like this. He really was missing a lot.

He was grunting hard behind her, both of them gasping near simultaneously as he slammed into her. Finally he pulled out of her and she turned around and fell to her knees and sucked on his prick.

"Let's take it downstairs," he said to her.

He helped her up and slapped her butt as they walked out of the room.

Down the stairs, she left him at the living room and said she wanted to get something in the bedroom. Shango sat on the long couch and waited with his prick in his hand listening to the rain grow heavy outside. Sally returned some seconds later with her cell phone in hand.

"Just wanted to check to make sure I didn't have any missed calls," she said. "Can't call Adam now 'cause he just arrived at work. Will take care of that later. Now, where were we?"

She was giggling like a school girl as she mounted him. The sound of the rain drumming against the window outside added eroticism to the sound of her voice as she sat on his cock and began to ride him. He allowed her freedom to do everything, except grabbing her ass and spanking it as she rode him.

"Spank me harder, Master!" she groaned.

He gave her a hard slap. She loved it; he gave her another and didn't stop slapping her butt as she kept on grinding and then bouncing down hard on him. The fabric of the couch groaned under their weight. Their lips caught each other passionately; their breathed into each other's face. Sally couldn't stop running her hands over Master Shango's features; she delighted so much in the feel and texture of his skin. It was like she hadn't met anything far more beautiful. She was climbing up the wall of her ecstasy and couldn't separate the difference between his prick fucking her or the warmth of his body pressed against hers. She ground her hips against him each time his hands smacked her butt cheeks.

"Awwhhh God ... You're so beautiful! Ahhh ... I want you to cum inside me!"

She slid her tongue in and out of his ear while she groaned against him. He had his hands under her ass cheeks and was lifting her up and bringing her down as hard as he could on his cock. His breathing was getting deeper.

"You want me … cumming in this pussy of yours, bitch?"

"Ohh yes, Master … it's your pussy!"

"It's my pussy, right?"

"*Your* pussy … Uhhgghhh … it's *your* pussy!"

He brought her to lie on her back on the couch. She rested one leg over the headrest while he brought himself between her thighs and shoved his cock back into her wet pussy. Her pussy made a squishing sound as he hammered down on her. Her pussy felt so good and so wet too. Shango quickened his pace. Sally brought both legs down over his backside. She was about to cum and couldn't wait to feel him pump his load inside her.

He could feel something racing down the length of his shaft. His face squeezed in emotive excitement.

"I'm going to fill your pussy!" he groaned.

Sally was moaning like cazy. Her body shook from the fit of exploding dynamite that went off inside her as she climaxed. Her face twisted in a rictus of hurting pain, but actually it was the sweetest ecstasy she could ever imagine.

"*GIVE IT TO ME …!*" She screamed so loud inside the house.

Seconds later Shango's body tensed and he grunted repeatedly as he spurt his load of cum inside her. He remained like that inside her for a while, letting every droplet of cum pouring inside her womb.

They got up afterwards and she made breakfast for them; it was approaching 11:00 am. The rain was still pouring although it had somehow reduced its downpour. She made tea for herself but coffee for him and they sat at the kitchen table naked and she wouldn't stop reaching across and feeling his arm while she did much of the talking. She told him about the places she'd love to take him to see down in the city.

They finished their breakfast and she then went and jumped into the bathroom. There was a Jacuzzi bath next to the shower stall and she mentioned to him about wanting him to try it with her and maybe fuck her inside it; Shango was game for everything and anything. He had finished putting on a shirt and pants and went back upstairs to conclude with the email he was typing while she took her bath.

She put on a flowery-type of dress that in his eyes complemented her complexion; as he'd wanted, she wasn't wearing any panties underneath. She called her husband and told him where they would be going as they locked the house. The sky still looked grey, though the rain was nothing more than a drizzle now.

Their home was in a suburban area and it took a while for them to get through the city traffic as they headed towards the Charleston harbor. They drove down Queen Street and as they approached they could see the view of the water. They were lots of tourists there, some street joggers running from one end of the harbor to the other. It took a while for them to find a parking space but they did and after locking up the car they strolled holding hands down the Waterfront Park Pier.

They ran into several couples there, all of them tourists. Sally gave them some advice as to moving around the city as well places to visit. She as well introduced them to her Black Master, telling them about what he was to her and how she's been so happy since he arrived in the city.

"Just visit his blog site, I promise it'll leave a lot of difference in your relationship."

***

Having seen much of the sight that was the harbor, they got into the car and drove away from the scene, getting back on the highway. Sally mentioned that she knew of a quiet spot where they could be alone. She was giggling when she mentioned this to him, and Master Shango, being the dominant figure he was, said they should make for wherever it was she had in mind.

They drove over the Arthur Ravenel, Jr. Bridge—she had been dying to show it to him—and went towards the outskirts of the city. She talked while she drove, telling him about how she and Adam had started having ideas of this lifestyle and of the numerous lovers she'd had in the past, some of whom was still itching for her even though she'd told them off not she had a Black Master in her midst. She never ceased to crack a smile and admire Shango whenever she mentioned his name in her gist. She periodically reached across her seat to touch him. She wanted to reassure herself that she was really with him and not a make-believe image. He too ran his hand over her thigh. One time they were in a traffic hold-up, he pushed her dress upward and licked a finger and inserted it into her cunt. She sucked in her breath. She opened her thigh more to allow him rub his finger around her clit and then gave her his finger to clean off. She sucked at his finger like she was sucking on his cock; she couldn't wait to have that one.

"You've got me itching with wetness," she moaned.

"Let's hope we get to wherever it is you're taking me so I can take care of that wetness then," he smiled at her.

He allowed her to drive. He looked out the window at the scenery they passed along the way now the traffic had let them through. The weather still had a dull outlook about it, and one couldn't tell if it really was going to rain or not.

Sally drove off the highway and took an exit lane which was like a lonely stretch road bordered by wild bush and trees; few cars passed them on the way. They took a couple more turns till they drove pass a wild grassy farmland country; on the other side they could make out the river with the distant bridge spanning it. Sally explained to him that years back she and Adam would try to get away from the kids to have some alone time together and would drive out here and have fun. She mentioned that it was a good picnic spot, and a lot of families during the summer do drive out here and as they drove, they caught sight of one or two families sitting on spread-out blankets enjoying the moment of summer.

She drove further past the field to a spot that had trees that bordered the river and parked her car in a spot that was remote from the road; anyone driving by wouldn't think twice of noticing them. They unlatched their seat belt and took turns crawling into the backseat; Shango had with him his iPod and he switched it on and played some music, though at a reduced volume to drown out whatever noise they were going to make but nothing else.

Shango sat down in the middle of the backseat and pulled Sally down to meet him. She was cooing with delight as she came and straddled him. Her hands caressed his face as her brought her lips to his; her lips parted and she sucked on his tongue and offered him the same. His hands pulled up her dress to grab at her bare buttocks which she ground against his crotch. Her hands worked at undoing his shirt buttons, gasping frantically against his face.

"I want you so bad, Master," she moaned.

Her hands pushed down her dress and his lips found her breasts and sucked on one of them. She came off him and both of them worked at freeing his belt buckle from his jeans. From where they sat they had a good view of the road and they both looked up when a car roared past them but went back to their business.

Sally licked her lips and her eyes gleamed with lust as she stroked Shango's cock in her hand; his cock gave off a throbbing feel as his erection hardened from her touch and pre-cum poured out the tiny slit on its head. She brought her head down and kissed the pre-cum before shoving inches of his prick into her mouth. Shango reclined himself and helped push his jeans and briefs down his thigh as she went on sucking him. She massaged his balls, her eyes were half closed and she moaned consistently in her throat as she felt his cock slip between her tongue and lips and her nostrils inhaled the masculine scent emanating from his crotch. He pulled back her dress and her voice groaned a higher note when he slipped his finger into her cunt; she raised herself on her knees to allow him further access. He pressed his other hand on the back of her head, forcing her face down more to eat his cock. She tried to take more of him into her mouth but obviously couldn't—his shaft was too much for her to ingest.

Shango kicked his feet out of his shoes and extracted them out of his jeans and briefs as well; Sally did the same and uprooted her dress over her head and except for her stocks was naked. Shango reclined himself further and brought her to straddle him once again, this time she remained on her high heels with her crotch hanging over his and her hands locked around neck and lowered herself down on him.

"Ohhhh … yes!" she moaned as she felt the head of his prick pierce her pussy entrance. She pushed her ass down his crotch, taking every inch of his cock, feeling her pussy expand as a result of his girth, then pulled herself up again. Master Shango too murmured a groan from the experience.

"Such a fucking good pussy!" he exclaimed.

He held her butt in his palm and lowered her up and down on his cock; pussy juice rolled out of her cunt and stained his shaft. Sally kissed his cheek. Her lips found his and she breathed into her mouth as they kissed fervently; her nipples were aching with arousal; the car rocked slightly and the scent of their sex now filled the interior. Sally's ass kept slapping down hard on Shango's thigh. She pushed her hair off her face and wouldn't stop moaning from the black cock pounding her. She brought her legs down and now rocked her thighs and hips back and forth. Her tits pressed against her Master's face; she held them up for him to suck on. Master Shango bit on her nipple, making Sally squeal with excitement. His hands slapped at her butt cheeks. His finger found her pussy hole and he thrust it into her anal hole and finger-fucked her ass while she went on bouncing and rocking her ass on his dick.

The music kept playing from his iPod. Vehicles drove past them as they kept on fucking. Sally was making wild noises in Shango's ear. Her pussy leaked her juice down his legs; the throb of his cock jamming inside her cunt along with his finger fucking her anus brought her climaxing and still she didn't want him to stop. She slid off him and he had her bent over on the backseat while he came at her from behind. She bit down on the seat's fabric as he pumped his cock hard inside her. Her cries were muffled by the fabric. Shango slapped at her butt, bent over her backside and worked his hips, giving her more and more of his prick.

He turned her over. He sat back on the seat and she straddled him again with her back towards him. His cock slipped out of her pussy and she reached downward for it and introduced it back inside her and balanced herself across his thigh while lifting herself up and down on his knees. She was groaning so loud now, rocking the car, as she was getting closer to having another orgasm.

Sally's phone suddenly came alive and was ringing.

Their eyes went to it. It rested halfway out of her handbag on the front seat. Shango told her to get it. Sally reluctantly leaned forward and got her phone and looked at the number and saw it was Adam calling. She told Shango who it was and he took the phone from her and answered it while she sat back on his thigh and returned his prick inside her cunt.

"Yo, what's up, white boi," Shango spoke into the mouthpiece.

"Hi there, Master," said Adam. "How're you doing? Is Sally there with you?"

"We're doing just fine, white boi. The bitch is right now feeling my dick. Here, I'll let you in on the action."

He handed the phone to Sally, who was back to moaning her pleasure once again. She took the phone from Master and spoke breathlessly into it. Her words were stuttered from the fucking she was getting.

"Ahh … hi honey … I'm … Uhgghhh … we're doing fine …"

"Babe … can I listen in?"

"Awwwhhhh yeah … sure!"

She let the phone fall from her hand and reclined forward. Shango had a great view of her buttocks now and loved it as she brought her ass down on him, taking his prick harder and harder. She would sometimes pause to grind her hips on his crotch and then resume slamming down repeatedly on him. The sound of their thighs slapping against each other, the sound of their breathing and their grunting voices all went into the phone where her husband was listening in.

***

Adam worked as a maintenance supervisor for a thriving wholesale equipment manufacture company. It was twenty minutes past the hour of his lunch break but he didn't feel like joining the boys to head out to Wendy's anymore, not when he had his wife moaning into his ear from wherever she was with her lover.

He left his desk and went to glance out hid office to make sure everyone had left. Feeling satisfied, he closed the door and turned the lock then returned behind his desk and unzipped his pants and played with his growing erection with one hand the other held his phone to his ear, listening to the moaning ecstasy of his wife getting fucked. How he wished he was there to see.

This was what he'd always wanted to see happen to Sally: her being seduced and being used by a *real* man. Used in more ways that he couldn't. How long it had taken him to come to this realization, and even when he did, it had taken quite a while for him to know what he really wanted. Years back, he and Sally had being involved in swingers lifestyle. They had enjoyed it at first, but had later become discouraged about it. The sex seemed so impersonal, and they'd gotten fed up with the sort of shady characters they often stumbled across whenever they'd been involved in any such mingling events. Another reason was that the kids had grown and left the nest, leaving them home alone with each other much of the time with little or no reason to play with others except stick with themselves, saying goodbye to a lot of assholes who'd been calling up their phone number wanting for a one-nighter with Sally. Sally's sexuality too had begun to dwindle and that he hadn't liked it at all. Age and deleted hormones. Not that he too was getting any younger. Hell, it seemed strange to him sometimes to wake up and realize that he and Sally weren't the young couples once they used to be. Their kids were now in their mid-thirties to early forties and they had aged into their late fifties and become grandparents. There was the house and the mortgage they were still working at settling, there was their frequent vacation trips they now had little time on their hands to be involved in ... and that was just about it. No other source of fun, nothing wild or adventurous to look forward to. He could understand with himself being the passive, hard-working creature he typically was, but Sally ... Sally had always had a thing for wild adventure and fun. She was his opposite in just about everything and he'd woken up and realized that soon enough she was turning to become just like him and he didn't want that to happen. No way, no how. He'd scoured through the internet, finding for some second life which they could both live with but it had been hard. The net was pretty vast, and a lot of times you run into people who talk more shit than reality.

But that had changed when he'd stumbled on Master Shango's blog page.

Reading through Master Shango's blog had opened his eyes and mind to things he'd never thought of before. Well, not that he hadn't thought of it, except that it was stuff he'd kept to himself, never once revealing them to Sally because he was afraid she'd think him crazy or worse that he was living too much in his fantasy.

Now here they both were, living the fantasy life that he'd always envisioned in a reality they could only have hopped existed. Master Shango had made things seem so easy and possible for him and Sally to achieve, and though at first when he began communicating with him, he'd opted not to get his hopes up. Not that he considered Master Shango and his teachings and tutelage as regards to cuckold lifestyle a hoax, but he needed to know he was dealing with the real thing and not some asshole making stuff up and posting them on the internet to lure people into a swindling-type of trap. They had communicated first via emails and then as the months went on, they'd exchanged phone numbers. At the time, Master Shango was home in Nigeria, he'd informed Adam of his impending travel to the U.S. and Adam couldn't be more joyful to hear it with the hopes that he would soon be closer to them and that in a few months time he was going to meet with this man, this demi-god who made cuckoldry so simplistic and wonderful for white couples around … and he was going to introduce him to Sally and love nothing more than for him to seduce his wife and turn her into a black cock slut as he'd always imagined she would be.

The proof was now in the making as he continued listening to them fuck over the phone while he kept playing with himself. He too was breathing heavy. He heard his wife climaxing and then heard her voice enquire to her Master if he too was about to cum. He made her know he was about to and Adam held the phone hard to his ear and most of held his breath for some seconds as he heard Master Shango groan loud enough for him to hear as he too climaxed. He could picture him cumming inside his wife's pussy.

It's too bad he wasn't there to watch them together; he couldn't wait for his day's work to be over to return home and catch whatever else they'll be up to.

He heard movement sounds coming from the phone, and then heard his wife panting into his ear, giggling.

"Hi honey, did you catch all of that?" she asked him.

"Oh yes, I did. Wow, looks like you're both having a wild time."

"Oh yeah," she chuckled. He could hear her panting breath and surmised the sex must have been an enjoyable one. "I bet you were playing with yourself while you listened, weren't you?"

It was his turn to admit. "You know I couldn't help myself. Is Master Shango there with you?"

"Yes, he's here. You want to talk with him?"

He didn't actually want to, but since she brought it up he figured why not. He head her pass the phone to her lover and then his voice came on: "How're you doing, white boi?"

"I'm very fine, Master. I was listening in on what ... you and Sally were having fun."

"Oh yeah, we sure have. She's been showing me around Charleston. Even talked to some tourists folks and told them about my website. You should have seen their faces when she mentioned to them of the magical stuff I can do. Anyway, we're here in some place she says you and her have been before to make out, and that's what we've been doing. Making out big time," he laughed; Sally too laughed as well.

They talked for a while they there hung up, saying they would be expecting him back home in the evening.

Adam dropped his phone and tottered out of his chair with his jeans handing halfway down his thigh and went into the small room in his office that served as his rest room. He closed the door and proceeded to jerk off inside the toilet bowl. The force of stream of his cum was like a jet plane taking off from a runway and he steeled his hands against the linoleum wall and groaned as he ejaculated his cum straight down into the bowl. He flushed when he was done and washed his hands and his face in the sink. He was feeling so good with himself when he returned to his office and pretended to return to work while his mind was wondering if Sally and Shango were fucking again or not.

Someone knocked at his door, startling him. He remembered he'd earlier locked it and he went and opened it and saw it was one of his junior workers who stood there with a take-out package from Wendy's. The younger worker observed his happy features and was curious as to whatever might be making his boss seem so happy today.

"Everything alright, boss?" he asked.

Adam looked at him and smiled. "Everything's just fine, Rob. Thanks for these," he indicated at the Wendy's paper bag. "Everything's fine as rain."

***

It was 6:45 p.m. and Adam was hurrying for home, trying to beat the city's late evening traffic. He spent much of the ride back reflecting on him and his wife and how far they had come with Master Shango's present visit.

Sally hadn't been an easy sell when he'd first let her in as to his communications with Shango four months back. She had thought it strange that he'd be spending wakeful hours in the middle of the night chatting and exchanging emails with someone who lived halfway across the world whom he hadn't yet met and knew little about. She had gotten even more upset when she found out he had been exchanging pictures with Shango of her without her clothes on. That part he'd had to explain much about. Sally still shook her head against it, though she didn't say it out loud, but she wanted him to desist from his activity. He probably would had it not being the encouraging words from Master Shango who'd prodded him from miles away of what he should do to win the wife over and the subtle tactics he should employ. Adam had done as he'd instructed him to do. He'd bought several of Master Shango's erotic books. They were fictional tales partly written from his experience with white couples and they mostly centered on white couples wanting to be dominated by black men and how basically of white people submitting to his might. The writing were outrageous, and charged with so much erotic imagery Adam got hard just from turning one page to the next. He'd read them all to himself once, then twice, before deciding to share them with his wife. Evenings when there was little for them to do, he whipped out one of Shango's books and read them to her. He took note of how disinterested she was at first, and later as he got further into the story he'd watched the grimness melt off her face. He'd finished one novel titled '*Mr. Tibbs*', and moved on to one he'd been saving for should she get the sort of reaction that she was having now called '*The Merry Wives of Black Master Shango*', and that had gotten Sally jumping so excitedly they'd made love in more ways than he could remember. They'd be in bed and he'd be reading the book to her with one hand holding it while he had the other rubbing her pussy and she'd slip his finger into her pink recess to feel how wet she was becoming. Adam had reported to Master Shango the ecstatic state his wife was in and when the time came, he'd prodded her to start communicating with Shango himself. She'd chosen to do it without further qualms on her mind and allowed Adam to take more recent erotic photos of her to forward to him.

Adam remembered the first time they'd spoken to him on the phone. That had occurred a month ago when he'd touched down in New York City. Master Shango updated his blog regularly and talked about some of the recent wives he'd met and conquered; Sally by this time was itching to be next.

Shango had been putting up with a friend in New York. He was opting to settle in the U.S. instead of traveling back home and was practically a 'fresh fish' trying to understand the intricacies of moving around in the U.S. He'd traveled down to Washington D.C. and settled into an apartment there. It was during this time that him and Sally began talking about wanting him to come down south and meet with them.

There had been skepticism on their part, but mostly from Sally. She'd fretted about her looks, her stature … almost every evening wondering how she should present herself to him. *What sort of clothes would he want to see her in? … what sort of panties? Would he find her attractive at her age? … would he find her sexy enough?* Adam had done his best to reassure her that Shango would appreciate her for being herself. She had written back and forth to him enquiring about this and he too had said the same thing to her: "Be yourself and don't be bothered. But don't wear any panties."

Adam couldn't have foreseen how well they would become with each other. That night they'd gone to meet Shango at the airport, Sally had been so feverish with excitement all through the ride that it had taken nerves of steel for him to calm her down. It was a good thing too because deep inside himself, he knew his wife was the most beautiful woman he'd ever set eyes upon, and it was his desire that any man out there, especially any black man like Master Shango, would see the beauty in her and be capable to want make her humble in bed. She deserves it more than he could give to her.

He arrived home just as the sky was getting dark; his wife's car was parked in the garage. He parked his right next to hers and felt like his body was taut like a wire as he came down from the car with his work satchel bag in his hand and went up the short flight of steps leading into his home; he stopped to caress the cat's fur before stepping inside.

It was dark inside the house as he entered through the kitchen door and for a minute he wondered if they were inside or not. He closed the door behind him and then heard sound coming from the TV, following by his wife's giggling laughter. He entered the room and found them curled on the sofa looking like two lovers enjoying their evening. His wife wore a black evening dress with high heels on. Her hair was tied behind her back and she had make-up on that made her glow the moment she turned to smile at him. She was resting against her lover's arm. Master Shango wore a tee shirt and jeans looking cool with a can of soda in his hand. They were watching a movie—*The Girl with the Dragon-Shaped Tattoo*.

"Hi there, honey!" Sally bounded from where she sat and came and hugged her husband. He wanted to kiss her but at the last moment she stopped him because she had on lipstick. "How was your day at work?"

"Was dandy," he said.

He dropped his satchel bag on a nearby couch as she led him to where Shango sat. He stood up and they shook hands. Adam went back into the kitchen and looked in the fridge and got himself a soda as well and returned to sit on the couch he'd dropped his bag.

"You two look like you're heading out?" he said as he popped the tab of his drink.

"I wanted to show him around some more," his wife remarked. "We were thinking of heading out to go watch a movie at that new theater they opened up on Broad Street. Why don't you come join us, it'll be good for you."

"I don't know if I could. I'm pretty tired from work and everything."

"We can wait," said Shango. "Best time to go watch a movie is always when its late."

"Nah, I wouldn't want to hold you both up. I'm just going to take a hot shower and go upstairs and type some reports before hitting the bed. Has she tried out the Jacuzzi with you?"

"No, we haven't had time yet," Sally answered for him. "But maybe tomorrow, we'll take a dip in it."

They went back to watching the movie. Sally rested against her Master's arm, her hand ran over his chest and his arm and she laughed each time he said something funny to her. Adam was enjoying the sight of watching them together. Sally looked so different right now, so young too, almost like when they'd first got married. He couldn't tell how long she intended to keep this relationship with Master Shango, and that was something that worried him. Not of his wife falling in love with him as a woman would with a lover, but if really he had any intention of wanting to keep her. Sally wasn't a young woman, and Adam wouldn't be surprised there'd be lots of lonely white women out there wanting Master Shango's expertise, wanting him to come and fill their pussy up just like he'd been doing with Sally. He reckoned that just like Sally was right now with him, those other women would be reluctant to let him go that easy. He's a nice enough guy, and Adam had met some men who claimed to be Black Bulls, but he figured much of them was all talk and nothing else; Shango appeared to be the real thing and if he ever had had doubts before, he knew he wasn't going to be having any as long as Sally remained this smiling and happy with him.

Adam got up and said he was going to have his shower. By the time he'd finished taking his bath and he came out drying himself, Sally was in the room checking herself in the mirror one last time before she and Shango went out. Adam came to her from behind and caressed her tits behind her dress; he loved the perfume she had on. Quite intoxicating. She giggled as he kissed her neckline.

"How're you doing, babe?"

"I'm doing just fine, darling." She turned around and hugged him. "I can't tell you how happy I am right now."

"Happy that your lover is here and he's everything you always wanted?"

"Yes, all of that. But also I'm happy that you're doing everything possible to make me happy, and I love you so much for that."

"Making you happy is what I'm here for, honey. You go out and have fun and tell me about it later, okay."

"I sure will. Catch you later, darling."

She rubbed his back then left him. Adam wore his robe and came out in time to see her pick up her handbag after she'd switched off the TV set. Shango stood up and pushed down his shirt and waved at Adam as Sally led him out of the living room. They went through the kitchen door and out of the house. Adam came into the kitchen and watched from the window as they got into Sally's car and reversed out of the driveway. He could still hear the sound of the car driving off as he turned away from the window and went to do something about the office reports he needed to take care of.

***

Sally was in high spirit as they drove away from the house and back into the city. She had her lover seated beside her, he was just as happy and warming being with her, nothing else could have made her feel more happy and excited as she was right now. She had promised showing him around much of Charleston and having as much sex with him as possible. Well, the sex part she knew she was going to get as long as he stayed here with them. And it didn't appear like he was growing tired of her at all.

They conversed as she drove. She told him about several of her friends whom she'd been conversing with over the past month, trying to convince them to try having a black lover. She told him about this one friend of hers whom she'd love to introduce him to. Her name was Gail, and she was much younger than her and has a white boyfriend who'd once talked about wanting to see her try a black cock before. Although she said her friend was going to require some convincing, but now he was here, she felt she could find the strength in her to do just that. She wouldn't stop thanking her Master for being with her, and for his sweet words he'd used to give her strength to carry on with this.

They arrived at the movie theater some minutes after the sky opened up and rain poured down from it. There weren't much people at the theater—it was nearing 10:00 p.m. and much of the movies had already begun to show. Master Shango was hoping to watch the latest Batman movie but the time indicated it was soon approaching its end. He and Sally opted to watch the latest Stallone flick, 'The Expendables Pt. 2'; the movie had begun less than five minutes ago. They paid their tickets and the usher lady told them which theatre door to go into.

The theatre room was dark as they pushed through the door and entered it; the movie was already playing as expected. Master Shango scanned the dark room and saw few people in it—he couldn't have liked it any better. He led Sally up the steps and they went to the top line of chairs and sat down beneath the projector window. Several chairs to their left two men sat watching the movie with them, though after a while they got up and left the room; now they both owned the top floor.

They watched the action-packed movie, although Shango had other things on his mind. He was caressing Sally's thigh while they watched and she too had her hand groping crotch, feeling the bulge that was getting harder inside his jeans. The movie was still playing; the few people that were in the room sat further down from where they were. Master Shango spread Sally's legs and she sucked air through her teeth and tensed up when she felt his fingers strumming the soft meat that was her labia lips. She was struggling not to whimper too much, but she knew that was a worthless affair. She couldn't hold back the tinge of arousal her body was feeding her. Her mind already was beginning to run riot and she brought her hand and grabbed at her breasts, feeling her erect nipples push against the fabric. She felt like opening her mouth and screaming out. She turned to her Master and plastered her lips to his and then she let loose her torrent of scream while kissing him as she felt his finger slip into her pussy. Her body was like a high-strung wire. Her hips were dancing with electricity as she pushed herself forward to capture more of her Master's finger to rolled in and out of her cunt. The volume of the movie playing was loud enough to help quell her ecstatic screams. Master Shango now had her partly facing him, fucking her pussy harder with his finger while he kept his lips glued to hers, listening to the sound of her moan while at the same time sucking on his tongue. He extracted his finger and gave it to her to clean up, which she did. By now she was gasping so heavy, yearning for more.

She murmured into his ear: "Please, let me suck your cock."

The space between his legs weren't that wide enough for her to kneel in front of him. Still he unzipped his jeans and she bent her head to suck on him. He sat back with his hand caressing the back of her hair, watching the movie that played in front of him. He took note of the few people in the room and of the doorway just making sure no one came up and surprised them. In a way he wondered what some of the folks might think if they knew they were up here having this sort of fun without them knowing. He wouldn't be surprised if another couple had before in the past tried such before.

He was luxuriating in the warmth of Sally's mouth engulfing his cock. He would have loved to fuck her pussy right here and now but knew it wouldn't be possible; perhaps next time he would ask her to take him to any porn theatre around and see if they'd have some room in there. She kept pulling at his cock with her mouth, willing him to shoot his load up in her throat. He pulled her face up and told her to suck him harder. She went back to her job and this time put in more pressure on his cock. He felt his hair trigger coming up gradually. He wanted very much to cum in her mouth. Minutes later, to his surprise, he did. He pressed her face down on his meat, felt her continue to scoop up his cum in her mouth. She licked up every trace of semen from his shaft and when his meat now became deflated, she sat up and kept playing with his cock in her hand, stroking him. They sat like that and watched the movie to the end. Shango's erection got back again from her constant stroking, and he kept on squeezing her thigh and she as well allowed him to feast on her tits as well.

The movie over, the lights came on and they came down the steps and left the room. They separated in the lobby, Master Shango went into the men's room and Sally too went to hers. They met each other back in the lobby some minutes later; it was still raining outside, although it had slowed to a steady drizzle. They ran under it and got into the car and drove out of the theatre packing lot.

***

It hadn't taken Adam much time to finish his report and turn his attention to other things. On his browser he clicked on the bookmarked button that took him to Master Shango's blog site. He saw that he had updated it earlier in the day. Adam sat back and read the posting he'd done about his present stay at his home here in South Carolina. He had mentioned Sally, but used a different name, and also he didn't mention the location where they resided. Master Shango had mentioned to him before of his discretion in his affairs and Adam felt reassured to see that he'd kept his word of never yet exposing Sally to the world. However he was thinking seriously about it. He sure wouldn't mind if people out there found out about them, learn more from them about the sort of lifestyle they're living and how happy it makes them feel. He reckoned a lot of couples out there would be just as surprised and happy to know about them and how they'd become part of Master Shango's harem.

He didn't know what was going to happen now: would Master Shango be planning on wanting more of Sally, or would he make this a one-time thing and they won't hear from him anymore. He'd love to spend time with him to get to know him more. It was just bad he was choked with work this point in time. He couldn't read every detail in his wife's mind but he was willing to bet a Dollar that Sally too was wondering the same thing as well. For years he'd been searching for this sort of lover for her to have, and now they'd found him, it was speculation as to how things would be with him. They were different now. A lot of changes in their lives, and with Master Shango, should he wish to still have them, there was bound to be further adventures the likes he knew Sally would be dying to have. One night he and Sally had talked about him moving into their home. It was something that had been brewing in his mind and that night as they talked about it in bed he realized that she too had been thinking about it as well. It sounded like a good idea—they had the house all to themselves, though they had lousy neighbours, but it wasn't their business what they did with their lives. Besides, with Master Shango here with them, they could have whatever sort of sexual adventure they choose.

It was a good idea ... but then Sally had brought up a question that seemed to nearly knock it off their mind: "What happens if the kids come to visit and they get to find out about him?"

Adam hadn't thought about it, and that night he couldn't think up an answer. They had four kids, all grown and married and though neither of them lived in South Carolina, they dropped by every now and then to spend a weekend or even a week with them. Neither could imagine how their kids might react to their Mom and Dad letting them in on their new lifestyle—it was even a miracle that they'd kept their earlier on swingers lifestyle from them, but that had been possible because majority of their meetings had happened out of state, never close to where they lived. But this involved them in their home. Sally had said to him that she didn't think if after meeting with Shango and finding out that he's the type of gentleman that she want that she would consider lying to her kids should they ask. Matter of fact, a lot of times she had thought of calling them up and letting them in on their secret but Adam had applied the brakes on her. His excuse had been their kids wouldn't know how to take it. Sally had argued against that, saying their kids were mature enough to make their minds as regards sex, and besides, this involved them alone and not their kids. Adam still had insisted it wasn't that good an idea. They'd talked about it, they'd talked around it, not finding a means of getting to a compromise, they'd decided to hold it off till they met with Shango, at least until they decide if he's the right type of fellow for her or not.

Adam watched some of the erotic videos he'd posted at his blog; he always checked on his blog almost every day to know if anything new had been added or not. He looked at the time on his system and saw it was less than forty minutes before midnight. He switched off his computer and turned off the bedroom light then went and laid on the bed. He didn't shut the bedroom door; he wanted to catch them when they return.

Master Shango and Sally returned at 11:46 p.m. Adam as just about drifting off to sleep when he thought he heard the sound of the kitchen door slamming close, followed by footsteps in the house. He pushed the covers aside and quietly got up from the bed and approached his door. He stood there and heard them talking downstairs. He stepped out his room and looked down from the balcony and there they were playing on the couch. Sally sat across his thigh and looked like she was riding him. His jeans hung down his legs. Adam watched as he groped his wife's ass cheeks. Sally was moaning louder now. She pushed her dress downward and allowed him to suck on her tits. Adams stood hidden from view and watched them. He was getting a boner underneath his robe. He loosened his robe and played with his erection while he watched them fuck. He listened to the rise and fall of his wife's cries and could only imagine how big Master Shango's prick might be as she rode him.

Sally came off him and helped free his jeans off his legs. Master Shango kicked off his shoes and made Sally ride him again. This time, having ridden him for a while, he got up from the couch, lifting her up and carried her towards the master bedroom. Adam listened to his wife's excited squeal as both of them disappeared from view. Adam stood there undecided for a moment, not knowing if to come down and watch them fuck or returned to bed.

Fuck the bed, he murmured to himself. Holding his erection in his hand, he trooped down the stairs to see what was going on.

There was Sally's voice clamouring fervently and high-pitched for her Master's cock; even if he'd been born deaf, Adam swore he would have heard her screaming moans. He came to the door and stopped and peeked inside, feeling like a child in his own home.

The room's light was on. Shango stood beside the bed and was fucking Sally from behind. He was pounding her with such force it got the bed to move some inches forward. She grabbed the back of her dress, pulling her back each time he slammed into her. Adam marvelled at the sight of her ass bouncing backward and forward to meet his dick. He saw the way her tits bounced as she leaned forward on the bed, saw the hurting, flushed look on her face that told him she was getting the best black dick ever; the moaning pleasure of her voice added further testament to that.

"Ohh God! Your cock … Uhhh your black cock feels so fucking good!" she sighed.

"You're going to be getting more of that black cock, won't you, bitch?" Master Shango slapped her ass.

"Awwhhh … Aww yes! Fuck me, don't stop!"

Adam stood there listening to the sound of his wife groaning with her face pressed on the bed sheet while Shango fucked her as hard as he could from behind; the sound of her ass slamming against his pelvis was undeniably intoxicating. He turned and saw Adam standing there by the doorway and smiled at him.

"Hey there, white boi. You enjoying the show?"

"I very much am," Adam responded.

Sally raised her face from the bed and motioned her hubby over. "Come, honey … Agghhh … come over here!"

Adam entered the room and went to her side of the bed, facing her. His prick was pushing forward against his robe. He held it open for her and she sucked on his cock while at the same time groaning from the pounding she was getting. She munched on her husband's cock and tugged on his balls. Adam groaned and pressed her head down on his dick; he hadn't been this excited in a long time and he hopped he could make it last. He grasped her tits with both hands; her mouth came off his cock and she groaned from it. She was struggling to fight back from the tightness she was feeling in her chest. The pounding she was getting from Shango's prick was too unbearable for her to take. Her body went to spasm and she stopped to breath from a second as an serious orgasm crashed into her. Her mouth grasped her husband's cock as if for dear life. Adam couldn't hold back his own and he poured his load inside her mouth. Shango was groaning and grunting harder now. When his turn came, he pulled out of Sally's pussy and made her turn around to face him. Sally came off the bed to be on her knees before him and he fed her his dick and grunted aloud as he pumped gallon after gallon of his cum down her throat. Sally ingested all of it and kept stroking his cock for more.

That night the three of them slept on the bed with Sally taking the spot between them. She reclined herself against her Master's arms. Adam loved the sight of them laying the way they did and when he slept, he barely knew it.

Day 3
Wednesday 29th August, 2012.

Morning came and were it not for the alarm clock ringing off, and then Sally pushing him forcefully awake, Adam probably would have slept all through the hour and forget he had work to go to. He jumped out of bed yawning and went into the bathroom to urinate and then jump in the shower. He came out of the bathroom minutes later with a towel around his waist and saw his wife curled in Master Shango's arms. He went about his business getting himself something to wear then went to the kitchen to get some breakfast. He told them he was leaving as he got his keys and left them still in bed.

Sally and her lover got up from bed an hour later and while they ate breakfast, she told him of the places she'd like to take him to, also about both of them stopping over at Costco where she could see about hooking with that friend of hers she'd mentioned to him yesterday, Gail.

She made breakfast for both of them, still feeling tired she returned to bed.

Shango went upstairs to his laptop and checked on how well his blog site readers were going with his postings. He'd received plenty of mails overnight, much from hubbies telling him about his wife and wanting to know if he could help them with seducing the wives and having his way with them however means he wanted. Shango was game for anything, but always exercised caution when it came to this. One thing he'd come to realize is how asinine and plain dumb a lot of them could be. Most times he couldn't tell if they were serious about what they wanted or whether or not they were jerking off too much to interracial porn and it had somehow clouded their thought process. He found it hard gauging their level of seriousness. Sure, he could tell they were honest with what they want and would actually give anything to see their wife being handled by a black man … the question was just how serious where they willing to go to see this dream become a reality?

Communicating with these type of people was often amusing at the same time a worthless endeavour. He would have appreciated it more if they ignored getting in touch with him for real. They should just read his erotic stories and article postings at his blog and jerk off to the videos he posted there and leave him alone.

He didn't know if he had time to post something—his body felt weary from the bout of fucking he'd been carrying on with all through yesterday. He himself was amazed at his prowess. He hadn't thought he'd have it in him to be able to carry on with this triathlon of fucking he'd been giving Sally from the moment her and her husband picked him up at the airport—My God, it felt he'd stayed a week now! He thought of what to write and got down to it. Minutes later he had written an 800-word article of how well he was enjoying himself down here in Charleston. He wanted to make it longer—he seldom enjoyed posting shorter pieces—but he was feeling pretty tired. He opted to leave it for now. He closed the lid of his computer and went downstairs.

Sally was still in bed. He would have loved to join her and see if he too could maybe catch a few winks but reckoned she might wake up once she heard him come to bed and then her sleep would be cut short—he reckoned they still had more fun to play with each other. He wore on his tee shirt of yesterday and went and laid on the long couch in the living room. He laid one arm over his face and pretended to fall asleep. He remained like that for a while then realizing the futility of it, got up and went to take a shower. The water washed the dregs of sleep off from his eyes and he was feeling pretty good when he came out and dried himself with a towel and after putting on fresh clothes returned upstairs to his computer and finished with the article he was composing and when he was done, he posted it online and closed the lid back, good to know he'd at least finished with that one.

He sat in the living room and watched some TV, though with the volume reduced, not wanting it to wake Sally up. He needed have bothered because minutes later she was calling out for him. He switched the TV off and went to meet her in bed; she hugged him like he was a missing teddy bear. They kissed and he played with her tits and she sighed and brought her body against his and laughed mischievously.

97

"What time is it?" she asked.

He looked at his watch. "10:38 a.m. You'd better get up, or else we're going to stay in bed till evening."

"Hmmm, wouldn't that be nice," she cuddled herself against him. "I can't believe what you've been done to me since you got here. I haven't had this much fun in a long, long time. Even if I had, I doubt it's been like this before."

"You ought to be having more fun like this. It keeps you healthy."

"I know. Just had too many things on my mind. I'm really going to miss you when you leave. I hope you'll return."

"Did you think I wasn't thinking about coming back?"

"No. I know we haven't talked about it, but it's something Adam and I have talked about. We even talked about you moving in here with us. He wants you to, but we're kind of worried about our kids."

"Yeah, that could get in the way. But let's keep our minds open about it—we needn't make it happen now."

"You're not upset about it, are you?"

"No, why should I be. The main thing is you and Adam now know me well enough and you know I've got your best interest on my mind." He squeezed her breasts while he said this and when he was done, took a bite of it. Sally cooed with delight and rolled over to be on top of him. Her hand slid downward to cup his groin.

"I think I'm waking the beast in your jeans," she laughed. "I want to take a shower, but I want you to fuck me in the bathroom, too."

"In that case, I'm going to take the shower with you." He came off the bed and removed his tee-shirt. "A second shower for me this time."

***

They were in the car driving out towards the city. The sky looked partly cloudy, though the weatherman on the radio had mentioned that it would rain further south of the state but not here in Charleston. Shango had checked the weather forecast in his computer and knew that there was a hurricane brewing in the Gulf of Mexico region and it was pushing some angry weather towards their direction; it was raining up in D.C. he saw.

Sally drove to the Costco location where she hoped her friend would be at. She couldn't recall her number and thus couldn't call her to know if she would be there or not. They went inside and she took Shango towards the clothing section of the big warehouse which was filled with all sorts of wholesale items. She ran into her friend Gail and introduced her to Shango. Shango left the women to chit-chat—he didn't want to intrude on their line of conversation when he already knew where it would be. He wanted to give Sally enough room to work her magic. He strolled over to where he saw books for sale and perused the ones that were there. His eyes fell upon 'The Girl with the Dragon Tattoo', and he took it with him. His phone rang and he saw it was his friend in D.C. calling to check up on him. He answered his phone while at the same time watching Sally converse with her friend from afar. He noticed them staring at his direction and turned his eyes away while he told his friend what a fun time he was having in the southern state.

Finished with his phone call, he paid for the novel and sat at a Subway snack-food stand and ordered two hotdogs and a soda. Sally came to meet with there, pulling her friend along. They shook hands again and Sally mentioned that Gail had a two-hour window-break from work but if they needed to be away, then it had to be right now. Shango wolfed down his hotdog and took his soda with him and then they left; Gail sat in the back while they drove for home.

Sally was careful keeping to the speed limit, even though she was so much in a hurry to get home with her two companions. Shango struck conversation with Gail. She appeared a bit cool speaking with him, but by the time they got close to home, she was laughing at his jokes. She asked him how he and Sally had met, and Shango told it how Adam had found his blog site and somehow they'd got to talking. Sally was laughing while they talked; she couldn't wait to show her friend what her Master was capable of. Gail mentioned her boyfriend and of him wanting to see her in bed with a black man and then how he'd changed his mind because he was afraid that she might get to enjoy it and end up leaving him. She was gushing and blushing while she said this.

"That's pretty sad about you and your BF," Shango said to her. "But how did you feel when he changed his mind about it?"

Gail shrugged, blushing. "Well, I guess it don't really matter now ... I was kinda upset about it. I mean ... well, we'd talked and talked about it, and then all of a sudden he pulls the plug on me doing it. I asked him about it and he just kind of pushes me aside at first, saying he didn't want to talk about it. At first I thought it was over and done with. Then two nights later I caught him watching interracial porn and that got me upset. That was when he told me his reason, and I got mad about him for it."

"Why? You got made that you found him watching interracial porn?"

"Yeah, it was the deal we had. I told him I was okay with him not wanting me to fuck a black guy anymore as long as he quit watching porn, especially interracial. He told he no problem with that, but then I caught him doing it, which means he's a cheeky bastard and I don't like that."

Sally laughed. "That was about the same way I too felt about Adam when he discovered Master Shango's blog site and then told me he'd been sharing my pictures with him. Got me mad too, but we handled it fine." She reached across to caress her Master's thigh. "If Adam hadn't changed my mind, I never would be enjoying the fun I've been having since Master Shango arrived."

They got back home and they went inside. Everybody took off their shoes before entering the living room. Master Shango sat on the long couch while Gail, still feeling shy at the same time expectant of whatever was going to happen, sat alone across from him. Sally got her a soda from the fridge before coming to sit in Shango's arms. She was gushing with excitement as she kicked her legs open. Gail almost choked on her drink when she caught view of Sally's naked pussy under her skirt.

"Now, where were we?" Sally said.

"Right where we ought to be, babe," replied Shango.

She sat forward and wiggled her bottom on his groin while he squeezed her tits from behind. Gail sat forward holding her soda in her hands and watched open-mouthed and shocked at what unravelled before her eyes. Master Shango pulled Sally's blouse up from her head, exposing her breasts in her bra; her bra came off not long after that. She came off him and turned around on her knees and he helped undo his belt buckle and push his jeans down his thighs while she stroked his prized cock in her hand and turned to wink at her friend.

"You see what I've been having?" she waved her Master's cock like it was a flag. "This is the best thing you can ever have in your life right now, Gail. Trust me."

She turned her head and sank her mouth on Shango's dick. Gail felt her mouth come unglued at the sight of what she was seeing. She was both amazed and shocked by her friend's actions. When Sally, back at the store, had told her of the great sex she was getting, she at first thought she was joking. Then she'd pointed at Shango and said she was going to make a demonstration of what they've been doing. She had come under the impression that it was all some silly hoax; it wasn't looking like a hoax anymore. Her ears weren't deceiving her as she caught the sound of Sally moaning in her mouth while her lips pulled on Shango's black cock. Her eyes weren't deceiving her either as her face bent over Shango's crotch and her hand stroked his shaft. Shango reached over her and pulled up her skirt, displaying her naked fleshy ass for Gail, and he licked his fingers and inserted them into her cunt from above. Sally wiggled her butt for him; her concentration remained on his dick.

"You enjoying the show, Gail?" Shango smiled at her.

Gail was speechless, not knowing how to respond or what manner she ought to. She could say nothing except continue to watch.

Sally came up for air. She pushed her skirt down her legs; Shango too removed his jeans and shorts and stood up and kissed her and caressed and slapped her buttocks. Sally looked like a child in his arms. She stroked his cock while he fingered her pussy. He brought her to lie on the couch and he knelt between her legs and ate her pussy. Sally squeezed her tits in both hands, her stomach undulated as her hips pushed upwards to meet his probing tongue. She cried out when he fingered her anus and kept on sucking on her pussy. She squirted and her body erupted in spasms.

Her feet kicked the air above Shango's head. Her body shook all over and she was gasping and crying at the top of her voice. Shango held her down. His face remained buried on her pussy, still finger-fucking her puckered hole while at the same time rolling his tongue over her pussy; she was squirting like a fire hydrant upon his face. Gail jumped to her feet, her eyes glued at what she was seeing.

Sally was hyperventilating and moaning like crazy. "Ahh … Awwhhh fuck! Awwhh fucking … fuck me, Master! I want you to fuck me!"

Master Shango was beating his dick before she even spoke those words and he shoved his dick between her pussy folds and right away her cunt swallowed his shaft. Sally groaned and her body stiffened as he sank his sword inside her. She grabbed hold of his arm and hissed through her teeth as she underwent another tremor. She was beating her head from side to side, driving her hair in a whirl across her face, gasping.

"Uuhhh God! Your cock … your black cock feels so fucking good!"

Shango drew her legs on his shoulder and worked his cock in and out of her pussy, loving the way her tightness squeezed his dick, loving the look of lust apparent in her eyes from what he was doing to her. He turned his head and saw Gail standing behind him with her skirt held up, rubbing at her panties; she too had a glazed look in her eyes like she was sleeping walking and didn't realize it. She edged closer. Shango wrapped an arms around her leg, feeling the smoothness of her flesh. He indicated at her to sit right next to Sally who barely knew where she was at that moment.

Gail held Sally's bouncing tits in her hands and fingered her nipples. She brought her face down and sucked on her breasts. Sally gave a solid moan from that; she held her friend's face to her tits. Gail's hand went downward to rub Sally's clit, touching Master Shango's dick, watching the way his pussy-coated black cock slipped in and out of her friend's pussy with ease. She was so intrigued by it; her eyes meet Shango's and he knew what she was thinking. He gave Sally's cunt one hard thrust of which she replied with a loud sigh and then pulled out of her.

"Come here and get some of this," he grabbed the back of Gail's head and pushed her face down towards his wet dick. "I know you want some of this."

Gail indeed wanted some of his dick. She took his cock in her hand and licked her friend's pussy juice off the tip of his shaft before applying her mouth to it. Shango muttered a groan as she swallowed inches of him. He rose to his feet and had both women sharing his cock, taking turns sucking him. Sally attended to his balls while Gail ran her tongue around his dick. Her fingers undid the top buttons of her blouse. Shango reached his hand inside, pushed aside her bra and cupped a handful of one of her tits; he did the same to Sally's breasts as well. He took pleasure in the sight of watching both women fight over his cock.

"How about we take things into the bedroom?" he said to them.

Sally smiled at her friend and said, "I think it's time you get to feel what I'm having."

Gail stood up and was out of her clothes in seconds except for her thong panties; she wanted to take it off but Shango motioned her not to. He led her into the bedroom while Sally stayed back to pick up their clothes. She took her cell phone as well and came to join them. She took several snapshots of Gail sucking on Shango's dick as he stood up on the bed. Sally remarked about how beautiful Gail looked and chuckled with the thought of what her boyfriend would say or how he'd react if he got to see his girlfriend right now. She came up on the bed and sucked on her friend's tits and fingered her cunt.

Shango took his cock out of Gail's mouth and laid on the bed, stroking it. He indicated for Gail to come on top. She was about to, but then stopped. A curious look lit her face.

"Wait, don't you have a condom or something."

Shango and Sally exchanged a look and then laughed.

"I don't use condoms, Gail," he said to her. "But I'm a hundred percent clean."

"He's clean, Gail," Sally reassured her friend. "Besides, he's not going to cum inside you."

Gail thought quickly. She'd never fucked another man before aside from her current boyfriend, and though this was cheating, the fool actually deserved it for leading her along all this time and then not giving her what she wanted. She saw it as divine justice. As to Shango not using a rubber ... she was partly worried about it, but the thought of refusing that black dick when right now every part of her wanted it was something she refused to pass over. She crossed one leg over Shango's thigh and mounted him.

She raised herself while Sally and her fought to insert his dick into where it ought to go, pushing her panties to the side. Her pussy opened and she shivered as she lowered herself. Her mouth uttered a cry as his cock penetrated her cunt and she sank down on it. She remained still, letting it simmer inside of her.

She began rotating her ass, squeezing her pussy muscles while she did. Shango as well pumped his thighs, pushing his cock all the way towards her cervix. The throb of his dick inside her cunt sent Gail floating towards the moon. Her tits bounced along with her; Sally came over and sucked on one of them. Gail leaned forward. Shango's cock slipped out of her cunt. Sally was there to clean his dick with her mouth before returning it into her friend's pussy.

Shango turned her over and came down and licked her pussy; Gail writhed on the bed; Sally came to her aid and sat over her face and offer her snatch to her. Shango got up and thrust his cock into her coochie and hooked her legs apart. Sally came off Gail's face. Gail held her legs apart and her pussy opened further for Shango to thrust his dick all the way. She was hollering, begging him to fuck her harder. Shango listened to the music of her cries; he raised a hand and wiped sweat off his brow. He grabbed her waistline and fucked her harder and faster; the sound of his pelvis slamming against her bottom went in sync with her moaning fit.

Gail was shaking head to toe. A climax was awaiting to ignite inside her. She could feel it coming and she boldly announced it. She pulled Shango down on top of her and held him tight, feeling only the movement of his hips pushing his cock deeper and deeper inside her. She too pushed her hips to match his fervour. She screamed inside his ear and almost at the same time she felt him about to cum. Shango withdrew from her at the last moment and sprayed his cum over her crotch. He made way when he was done for Sally to scoop the load of cum into her mouth.

***

Evening came.

Adam returned home from work tired but at the same time happy about hearing from Sally earlier on of Shango fucking Gail; she'd forwarded him pictures too. It was unfortunate they couldn't fuck one more round as Gail complained that she needed to be back at work soon. She'd had enough time to clean herself up in the bathroom after which they'd dressed up and driven out to return her at the Costco building. She had exchanged phone numbers with Sally and Shango and promised to keep in touch with both of them. She gave Shango a final kiss before stepping out of the car; she was looking forward to the next time he returned to Charleston.

Sally spent that night with Adam, leaving Shango all alone with himself in the master bedroom. She told Adam that Shango had said he wanted to return to Washington D.C., the next day. Neither was happy about it, but they were more relaxed now they know him and they talked about inviting him over when Adam would have a month's leave from work.

She as well promised that next time he came by, she won't forget to try out the Jacuzzi with him.

Shango returned to D.C. on Thursday and got to work uploading the pictures and videos he'd recorded onto his blog.

Persuasion

My wife's name is Jean, and the love I have for her is so grand I seldom cease the opportunity to show her off to anyone. On this particular day I was having lunch with a workstation buddy of mine named Reggie, and it was the day that marked a change me and my wife's lifestyle.

It was a Wednesday afternoon with the onset of early summer blooming around us. We were at a cosy restaurant not too far from our work office building and Reggie was over by my work cubicle giving me a word-for-word replay of last night's NY Yankees' game when my phone started to ring. I took it out of my pocket and smiled when I saw the person calling. It was Jean. I excused Reggie and took the call.

"Hi, babe," I spoke into the mouthpiece.

"Hi, darling," her voice floated into my ear. "You having lunch?"

"Yes, I am. I'm here with Reggie. Remember him?"

"Yeah, I remember him. Say hello to him for me, will you?"

"I'll certainly do that."

Jean and I talked for a while then we said our goodbyes and hung up. I was barely aware that Reggie had taken a pause to listening partly to our conversation. As for me, I smiled at him sheepishly and said, "That was the wife. Said I should say hello to you."

Reggie looked at me with a knowing smile. He was a black man in his mid-thirties. He was all bulk and muscle, much of which he'd achieved during his pro-football days back in college, and handsome too. At the office, a lot of the ladies often flirted with him, and he'd related to me several of his sexual accomplishments, though he'd never mentioned any known names to me. He was a cool fellow and I always enjoyed his company. I know if it weren't for the fact that I'd been a steady husband for the past four years, I probably would still be staying out late at night guzzling beer and trying to hook up chicks every Saturday night.

Only problem was I was never wired like such.

My life, you could say, I've always played it like a straight line. Back in college I was always the studious fellow always minding my business and hitting the books to care about social life or any benefits that came along with it. Though I wasn't overtly nerdy or book-wormish, I just didn't hang out much. Somewhere between the hours I wasn't reading and the few times I had to stroll into a neighbouring bar that wasn't that far from the college grounds that was where I met Jean. She'd been studying for a Major in Psychology. We spotted each other inside the hall and I bought her a drink and we made conversation and one thing led to another, we exchanged phone numbers, I introduced her to my few friends and she too did the same to hers, though we kept to ourselves often. I still remember the first time I made love to her. My heart was beating fast against my chest while I helped undress her. She too had been just as nervous as I was; later I got to find out that I was her first permanent boyfriend, not her first lover though. That one had been like a breeze in her life. It was a night neither of us would pull away from and since then, we've been together and now happy with each other in marriage.

As for Reggie, I can't help not admiring his style of living. He was an affable type of fellow, very charming and charismatic too. The type of guy who just lights up a room from the minute he walks into it. If you didn't know him, you'd think he'd been a movie star or something because he's got that charisma. I guess my liking him was partly the reason why I talked about him so much to Jean. Sometimes she would kid me about him, act jealous whenever I brought up any subject about him, claiming that I tattled a lot about Reggie she was scared I would soon be partying out with him and leaving her behind to cry her eyes out. I kept reminding her that's never going to happen. Who was I to know that the opposite was going to be the case for her?

Between Reggie and I, our conversation had often consisted of mundane topics: football games, gossip going on around the office, whatever we found shocking on last evening news … pretty mundane, typical stuff. But that we I answered Jean's phone call in front of him was more like the turning point in our friendship. Suddenly I wanted to talk to him about Jean, and that was what I did for the next forty minutes we were at the restaurant. He asked me typical stuff: how she and I had met, our future plans towards having kids and settling off the mortgage … then he went into a territory I never before then expected he would enter.

"How's the sex life like?" he asked me almost casually, like it was any typical question he would ask, except the look in his eyes told me it wasn't.

"It's fine," I replied, surprised that I was even deigning to answer his question when I should have told him that such wasn't any of his business. "We get to make out at least twice a week."

He looked at me oddly. "Did I just hear you say twice a week? That's pretty low for a sex life. You guys need to be hitting at each other every day of the week. That's how I would."

"Well, we all can't be a he-man like yourself, now can we?"

He shrugged at this and was silent for a moment, then he made a come-back. "Ever thought of making out some alternative means?"

I had no idea what he meant, at least then I didn't. "I don't follow," I said.

"You got a picture of your woman, I'd like to see what she looks like."

I told him I have a couple of photos of her stored in my computer system back at the office. We finished our lunch then returned to our office building.

Most of our co-workers hadn't yet returned from lunch. Reggie and I approached my work station cubicle and I opened my desktop computer, sifted inside my photos section and tapped on a folder I'd given a designated name. Hidden within the folder was a collection of Jean in various erotic poises. Some of the photos were a few months old; the recent ones were taken a week ago. There was her half naked in different pair of open blouse and others of her in tight jeans, there were some of her wearing garters and stockings and playing with her dildo in bed. Some showed her giving me a blow-job; those were my favourite. I looked at Reggie and the look in his eyes told me he loved what he was looking at. For me I was just as happy and swell with pride that finally I had something that's arrested my friend's attention. It wasn't until that moment that I realised the enormity of love I have for my wife and how much I loved showing her around for others to see. Of course that day was the first time I'd let any other pair of eyes aside from mine to view pictures of my wife's naked feature, it wasn't the last. Since then till present I've become more of a voyeur to Jean's sexual escapades. Though I never realised I would become a sub because of it.

I opened up all the pictures for Reggie's viewing pleasure. All in all, there were close to thirty snapshots of Jean in various erotic poises; Reggie though paid more attention to the ones that had her smiling and playing with her dildo in front of the camera. When we finished going through the collection it was with a heavy sigh that he looked up.

"Damn, bro, that's a hot-looking bitch—I mean, wife you've got there. Sorry about that."

He patted my shoulder but I was unmindful of his words. In fact they got me swelling even more. I couldn't help but Reggie fucking my wife and after he left me and returned to his work station the image of him and my Jean together kept running in circles inside my head. I probably would have mentioned it to him somehow if he hadn't made the move when he called my office number an hour later.

"Yo, man, I can't help it," he said to me as we spoke through the office phone. "Your wife is so damn fine. I can't get her off my head. I hope that ain't a crime with you."

I couldn't help but laugh from the excitement that came from his voice.

"No, Reg, it's not a crime. I'm happy you like her."

"I do indeed. Though I was wondering if I can get to see her in person. Maybe we could meet out for dinner or something like that. What do you say?"

I had to pause for a moment. Prior to when he called me I too had been thinking exactly the same thing, about asking Jean if I could invite a friend over for dinner. Jean had always complained that I never brought anyone home with me at all. And now here was Reggie taking the words right out of my mouth before I'd even declared them.

"I'll have to run it down with Jean first," I said. "I hope you don't mind."

"Oh yeah, sure, you do that. Get at me as soon as you can about it though. I'd really love to meet her in person."

"Yeah, I can easily tell from the sound of your voice," I laughed.

I took the subway train back to the district where I live; I do have a car but usually Jean and I make do with whichever of us is seriously going to make use of it for the day. It was about sunset when I arrived at my house and smiled when I saw our Hyundai parked beside the curb. Jean was inside cooking up something in the kitchen. We kissed and shared anecdotes of how our individual day had been. She was wearing a pair of summer shorts and tank-top with her tits bouncing with each movement she made around the kitchen.

We had dinner and later when we sat in the living room watching a TV drama and sipping beer I told her about my friend

Reggie and of her pictures that I'd shared with him. Jean at first was shocked, and I quickly had to calm her down and tell her that Reggie wasn't the sort of fellow who blabbed. For some reason she seemed to quiet down when I mentioned to her that Reggie was black. I took out my cell phone and showed her a snapshot of myself and Reggie with several other of our work colleagues. I told how happy and excited Reggie had been when he'd viewed her photos. This caught her attention very much. She leaned against me while I told her all what Reggie had said to me about her sexy body.

"My God, he actually got called me a bitch?"

She had one leg crossed over my thigh and was rubbing her hand over my arm and shoulder.

"Not really. I guess he didn't know when it slipped out his mouth, but he did say that."

Seconds later we were kissing each other. Our kissing got passionate and I pulled her over to sit on top of me. I pulled her tank top off from her head and she did the same to my t-shirt. Minutes later we had stripped naked and she had her mouth sucking my cock. I was gasping and sucking my breath while she went to work on me.

I struggled for my next words. "He wants … he wants if we could have dinner together."

Jean stopped in her sucking and looked up at me, stroking my cock.

"He said that? What did you tell him?"

"Yes, he did," I nodded. "I told him I would talk it out with you first."

I knew what her answer was before she mention mentioned it.

"Yes," she said. "Let's have dinner with him. Call him up later and tell him so."

She bent her head and resumed sucking my cock. I sat up on the couch and held my breath and struggled not to cum too quick as

I usually did whenever she decided to blow me. Jean had a lovely pair of lips and when they were wrapped around a cock, they could work wonders. So far the only cock they had been wrapped around was mine. For years I'd been praying for her to work those pair of lips on someone else and now with my friend inviting us to dinner and she accepting, I reckoned it wouldn't be long before that dream came about. I simply couldn't wait.

Later that evening while Jean was in the bathroom having a shower I called up Reggie and told him yes, we would very much love to have dinner with him. The day was a Thursday. We decided to fix the date for Saturday, he would be the one treating us.

The evening arrived and before I left for home, Reggie told me the name and address of the restaurant where we should meet up with him and what time he'll be there. Jean was just as excited as she'd ever been when I arrived home. She couldn't wait for me to tell her more news about Reggie. I was going to bottle up for a while to hold her in suspense but she held me at the front door and asked what, so I told her. She screeched like a nubile cheerleader and jumped into my arms and kissed me. Would you imagine, we hadn't yet talked about anything regarding what was going to happen after she and Reggie met yet from the way things went, we didn't need to. Things were already decided whether I liked it or not. We went upstairs and I sat on the bed to remove my clothes but she stopped to unzip my pants and pulled out my erection and brought her mouth to it. The fact that I was a bit tired and yet I came with such surprising force I never knew I had. We ordered Chinese take-out that night and stayed in bed eating and then making love. Even while we made love not once did I or she mention my friend's name. It wasn't necessary because we both sensed that he was there in bed with us.

Saturday came and as the evening got dark, Jean and I prepared for our date. I tried to look dapper in a suede jacket and jeans while my wife wore an evening blouse and skirt. Her outfit looked fitting for just the right sort of dinner outing we were bound to have. She wore her favourite pair of ear-rings which I'd bought her when we did our honeymoon in Cancun. What sealed the deal was that she wasn't wearing any bra behind her blouse.

As we got into the car and I drove towards where we were to meet with Reggie, the scent of my wife's perfume wafting over my face, I kept stealing glances to her lovely legs, seeing the way her skirt rode up her thighs. As I drove, I stole my hand between her thighs and caressed her skin, felt the heat warm my hand and how good it felt to hold her. She replied suit and felt her hand over my crotch and smiled as she felt my cock nodding inside my jeans. We shared a look and a second later burst into laughter. I took her hand in mine and brought it to my lips; we needn't say more than what we felt.

It was a trendy restaurant that Reggie asked that we meet him at, the sort where you'd have to book for a table at least a week early; Reggie must have gone all out to impress Jean for it. He was waiting for us in the bar and I led Jean forward and did the introductions. I stood a foot back to gauge their meeting. It was like watching two planets collide. Reggie shook my wife's hand and raised it to his lips; Jean was just as overwhelmed with meeting him and her cheeks turned crimson from it. We went in the direction of the restaurant where our table was waiting.

It was almost like I'd been delegated towards observing the two of them together from the moment we sat down at our table. Unconsciously without thinking of it until afterwards, I realised Jean was sitting close to Reggie by his right arm while I sat halfway across the table from them. It had an ironic twist like they were the ones on a date and I was a mere standby listening to their conversation and laughter; their eyes never once left each other to look in my direction.

"You're so beautiful, Jean," Reggie complimented. "Your man here told me how beautiful you are. Seeing you now, you're more of a goddess."

"Ohh, I'll bet you say that to just about every girl you meet," my wife blushed.

"I wish. I don't get to meet women anymore."

"You don't have to be modest about it, reg. My husband's told me a lot about you."

"Really?" Reggie glanced at me humorously; I couldn't help but laugh. "I hope he told you the juicy parts and not the bad side of me."

"Actually," her blush seemed to deepen as she choked on her words. She reached for my hand and gave it a squeeze. "He did whisper a bit about your bad side to me," she blurted then stopped, too embarrassed to speak further.

Reggie got the hint.

"How about you lean closer and whisper what you said to me so your man here won't hear," he suggested.

Jean leaned closer to him, enough for Reggie to train his eyes down the front opening of her blouse. He smiled at me in a conspiring way while my wife spoke hurriedly into his ear. He was grinning by the time she withdrew, and she once again turned her face away from him and squeezed my hand. Reggie's grin turned to laughter and he looked at me and said:

"You've been a naughty boy, filling your woman's head with crazy stuff. I'm ashamed of you."

My best bet was that Jean had told him what I'd once told her, about Reggie being a playboy who often boasted about his thick manhood. I played along and acted unruffled by their exchange. Listening to them converse was doing my cock a lot of good as it kept nudging against the top of my pants so hard I had to adjust it so as not to keep being uncomfortable by it. As we ate our meal, every now and then Reggie would whisper something into my wife's ear and she would respond with a blush flowed by a burst of giggles and whisper back at him as well. We were having so much fun just being there together and I almost felt disappointed when the time came for us to make our leave. Reggie whipped out a credit card and settled the bill. Jean got up and went towards the direction of the ladies room. Reggie indicated that I come closer. I pushed my chair over and leaned closer to hear what he had to say.

"No disrespect," he said to me candidly, "I want you to know your wife is going to be mine before the evening's over."

He didn't bother to hear what I had to say about this; he pushed me back to go seat in my former place, which I humbly did. The matters of the night were out of my hands.

Jean returned from the women's room still glowing like a radiant sun and we got up and left the restaurant. As we walked, Reggie and her locked hands together and conversed with each other while we waited in the lobby for the kid to fetch us our cars. I stood by myself and when our cars arrived, Reggie, without even a word to me ushered Jean to his and after closing her side door for her as he came round to his driver's side told me to follow him behind. He jumped into his vehicle with my wife seated beside him and drove off with me tagging some feet behind with no idea where we were heading.

We drove for a while then got to a red light. I sidled my car beside them and was kind of baffled when I didn't see Jean in her seat except Reggie seated on his driver's side. I raised my head to look closer and then caught a view of her bare shoulder which was sort of moving up and down. Reggie turned to look at me and smiled. Seconds later my wife raised her head from where it was hidden and adjusted herself in her seat, turned to look at me, rubbing her hand over her mouth like she was getting rid of a stain; she waved at me. To say I was startled that she'd just been sucking Reggie's cock was no surprise at all, except that she hadn't wasted time at all.

The red light went off and we kept driving.

We arrived our impending destination—a night club on the south side of the city; there was quite a large crowd outside all piling to get inside with bouncers guarding the entrance. I was never a club fellow and always felt socially awkward when it came to me venturing to such places. With Reggie in tow, I reckoned I was going to do just fine. We found a place to park our cars a block away then walked to the club; Reggie seemed to be a regular as we got inside with less trouble.

There was a hell of a party going on inside: lots of bodies dancing and grinding and milling about the dark interior with lots of roving lights, conversation going on everywhere, drinks flowing and little space to walk in-between. The music was pumping as we pushed past the throng of young people on the dance floor and found ourselves a corner booth that appeared somewhat hidden from view yet advantageous for us to see what was going on at the dance floor. Reggie and Jean sat next to each other while I faced them. We ordered drinks—the bill was on me—and drank to our health.

I ordered another round of drinks and while I sipped mine I tried to take my eyes off Reggie and my wife but simply couldn't. Reggie drew Jean's face towards his and they shared a long kiss. His hands rubbed at her arm and she brought hers to his crotch. I watched with excitement as she lowered her head and unzipped his pants and pulled out his cock and into her mouth it went. Neither of them cared where they were and I acted the role of a sentry, checking around to make sure no one was coming by our booth to check what we were doing. I was grabbing at my erection inside my pants while I watched my wife blow my colleague friend inside a nightclub. Jean pushed down the top of her blouse and Reggie caressed one of her tits while she continued swallowing his cock in the midst of the noise that was all around us. I was seeing my wife in a different light and from that moment on, the erstwhile image I'd always had of Jean melted away before my eyes.

Reggie came inside her mouth and I wish it were daylight and I had a camera right then to take a snapshot of her consuming his cum as a copious amount of it dribbled off the side of her mouth. Reggie pressed Jean's head downward and I watched as she sucked and swallowed every drop of semen his cock gushed into her mouth. When she was done, she gave his cock's head one last kiss before tucking it back into his pants. She wiped some off her chin and looked at me with a sort of 'I-Dare-You-Say-Something' sort of look. Of course I was too dumbfounded to even utter a word. I simply reached for my drink and downed its contents.

Reggie and Jean excused themselves from me and together they went and danced amongst the crowd of revellers. I ordered another round of drinks and tried to search them out from amongst the dancing floor crowd from where I sat but couldn't make them out. They returned sometime later and all through we stayed for more than an hour before deciding to take our leave.

Reggie and Jean walked ahead of me along the dark street as we made our way down the block towards where we'd left our cars. I followed them behind and watched with excitement and amusement as Reggie placed his hand on my wife's butt and kept grabbing at it. We got to where we'd left our cars and Reggie asked for my car keys. Without a word I gave them to him.

"Keep watch, white boi," he ordered me while he and Jean slid into the backseat and closed the door.

I leaned against the hood of the car and within minutes felt the car moving under me. I peeped through the side window and thought I could make out the silhouette of my wife riding my best friend; I could even hear the sound of her moans rising and falling with the car's movement. A trio or party people went past us; I waved at them and made like I was enjoying a fine evening with the sound of sex went on inside my vehicle. I wasn't checking my watch to know how long it went. When finally the door opened, Reggie slid out first and helped Jean out the backseat. She was fighting to put her clothes together. They returned to Reggie's car and once again I followed them as we drove off into the night.

We took a different route from that which we'd come and it occurred to me as we drove along that we were heading towards our home; Jean probably was leading the way for him. My heart was skipping beats at what the night was going to present.

We arrived at our compound and parked our cars in front of the driveway. Reggie and Jean got out and they were laughing as I led the way to the front door. I opened the door for them and closed the door after they'd stepped inside.

My wife kicked off her shoes while at the same time she flung her arms around Reggie's neck, kissing him with such passionate frenzy as I knew she possessed. His jacket slipped from his arm to the floor. I went and picked it up and draped it over couch as they fell down on a couch. Reggie slid his hand into her skirt and pulled her panties halfway down her thighs and then ripped it off her flesh. Their lips still locked on each other, kissing like crazy, his hand dove between her legs and I sat across from them and watched my wife squirm and moan from whatever Reggie's fingers were doing to her. He pulled her up from the couch and brought her across his thigh, his hand still strumming whatever guitar chord it were doing inside my wife's pussy, driving her wild and stir crazy while she pressed herself against him. I hardly knew when I unzipped my fly and freed out my cock and was stroking it while my eyes remained glued on them. They went on with themselves, totally not minding if I was there in the room with them or not.

Reggie freed his lips from Jeans and saw where her hand was busy grabbing at.

"You want a piece of that black cock, babe?" he asked her.

"Oh yeah," she purred. "I want it since yesterday."

Jean slid off his thighs and Reggie helped undo his belt buckle while she unzipped his fly and I observed the look of immense joy that lit up her face when she extracted the thick, black mamba snake Reggie had all this while hidden in his crotch. Jean was agog at the sight of his cock oozing pre-cum off the tiny aperture on its swollen head, and so too was I. I always reckoned Reggie had a big cock, but seeing it so up-close was like saying the Statue of Liberty wasn't all that tall.

"You like what you see?" he leered at my wife as if he already knew what her answer would be.

"My God, yes! Yes, I do see!"

Jean was drooling in her mouth as she kept waving his shaft inches from her face. She came forward and rolled her puckered lips around his swollen head. I watched with mounting surprise as she widened her mouth to take more of that black cock down her throat; Reggie's hand came down on her head, urging her downward. With one hand pumping his shaft, her other fondled his balls while her mouth remained busy dripping her saliva down his wet glistening skin. Reggie reached behind Jean and smacked her butt cheeks underneath her skirt. She muttered a cry from the contact and though it sounded like the crack of a whip, it merely spurred her onward. Her head went up and down on his shaft as gradually her mouth seemed to become used to his girth. Reggie pumped his thighs upwards, driving his thick manhood up my wife's throat. She choked repeatedly from it and yet the look in her eyes told me she was having fun.

Reggie kept pressing her head down on his crotch, groaning from her mouth's action. His thighs kept thrusting his shaft upward into her gagging mouth.

"Ohh yeah!" Reggie gasped. He couldn't stop squirming from what my wife was doing to him.

The moment came when his cock exploded in my wife's mouth with his load of cum. Jean's mouth seemed to expand from the tide flood. She choked on some of it while she fought to ingest every drop, spilling some of it on Reggie's thigh. She was about getting up but Reggie grabbed her hair and forced her face down on his crotch, snarling at her.

"The fuck you think you're doing, bitch? Lick up every drop of cum you spilled."

Jean did as he asked, obediently lapping her tongue over his thigh's skin. Licking up every drop of cum that stained his pants as well. Finished, she sat up and her hands frantically worked to undo the buttons of her blouse. Reggie too busied with taking off his shirt and the rest of his clothes; his cock stood erect at half mast over his thighs. Casting away his shirt and kicking his feet out of his pants, he impatiently pulled my wife towards him, not waiting for her to get out of her skirt. He brought her to sit across him, her legs straddled his thighs. They shared a kiss while Jean's hand went down under her legs and stroked Reggie's cock before inserting it into where it meant to call home. Her body stiffened as the head of his prick entered her. I heard her unleash a gasp; my eyes seemed to bulge at the sight of her perfect white globe of ass cheeks as she impaled herself down on my best friend's cock.

"Uhhhggghhh! Awwhhhggg, my God! Oh my God!"

My wife wailed as she came down hard taking more and more inches of Reggie's stupendous-looking prick. She leaned forward over his head and began wiggling her butt down on his thighs. Reggie's hands grasped her ass cheeks and he raised them up and slammed them down hard on his cock. It brought a sensational howl from my wife's lips. Her body jerked and responded to the slamming fit she was getting. Reggie was in control of the situation; I watched my wife surrender to her wanton lust as soon she found some courage to fight back and began bouncing her ass cheeks on him. Reggie slapped her buttocks hard each time she came down hard on him. He sucked on her titties at the same time jerked his thigh up and down under her ass cheeks. Thick cum juice dripped out of my wife's cunt. She was so wet I reckon it was only a matter of time before she announced her cumming.

Reggie and my wife retired upstairs; I followed behind, picking up their discarded clothes from the floor. In the bedroom, Jean threw me a blanket and a pillow and told me to make myself useful; Reggie sniggered as I undressed and spread the blanket beside the bed and laid my head on the pillow while they took control of the bed.

The fucking went on through the night. Sometimes I sat up to watch them and other times I laid on the floor jerking my cock while I imagined in what way they were fucking. Jean's cries filled the room, along with the creaking bed and then Reggie ordering her what to do. Sometimes she moaned his name. She told him how much she loved his cock and when he pounded her she frantically begged him to make her cum once more. I listened to her moaning voice as I would my favourite Beethoven CD. It was a symphony unlike anything I'd imagined. I shot my load in my hand and rubbed it off my thigh with the blanket.

I didn't know when I fell asleep. The room was dark and for a while there was silence. The silence broke when I heard Jean muttering in a low voice to her new-found lover, then what sounded like her mouth blowing him. A minute later the bed resumed its creaking noise and Jean's voice rose as I knew Reggie was fucking the shit out of her once more.

Rochester

Had me some fun time this past week:
I finally got to get my blog registered as a domain. Of
course that don't mean much, except soon it's going to stop having
that 'blogspot' in front of it and will then become a '.com'. I'm still
in denial as to how far I intend running with it. Think about it:
what's going to happen if someday I decide to run for public office
and then some reporter finds out about this web site? Imagine
the type of scandal that would bring. Of course, it's not going to
give me the type of fame former Senator Edwards has … but you
never know and you can never tell. Of course I'll still be writing.
Erotica's in my blood, and as long as there's hot wives out there
that need some satisfying and some hubbies too who just love the
sight of seeing their wives being made into a slut … I'll fucking be
there.

Anyways, Thursday came around and I had to take me on a trip
to Rochester in upstate New York. There's this white couple there
who've been keeping tabs and steady communication with me
back when I was in Nigeria. Now I'm in the U.S., of A, I figured it
time I paid them a visit.

I hopped on a greyhound bus and rode the journey for eight
hours till I arrived there. Rochester is a lovely city. Although
I didn't have much time exploring the city but you could tell it
wasn't bustling with the vibrancy that is new York City, at the
same time it's no quiet spot either. The couple I was supposed to
meet (let's call them the Morgans) reside in the suburb part of
the city called Henrietta. I got myself a cab and called the hubby
who gave me directions to a motel called the Super 8 on LeHigh

Station Road. I checked in there and gave the couple a call to let them know I'd arrived, just as promised. Of course neither was able to come visit me that evening cause of work and family, we decided to schedule things for the following day.

Aside from them, there was this other couple whom I was supposed to meet. The hubby wrote me a mail to come look for him and the wife at some eatery spot, but the fool neglected giving me his phone number, like he expected me to arrive there and from the description of what he and the wife would be wearing I would then guess it was them. I did call up a taxi and it drove me down to where they were supposed to be, but I couldn't find them and it pissed me off 'cause there I was looking like a fool trying to find a couple whom I couldn't tell from the crowd that was there. I got back to the motel and wrote a scathing email to the hubby and then went to a gas station next door and got some beers to end the night with.

I got a call from the hubby, Josh, the following morning. He called to say that he and the wife would be dropping by the motel to spend time with me later that evening. I told him that was just fine with me, I can wait. Later in the day I got a call from the wife, Michelle. She was at work at the time, though took the time to sneak out of her office to give me a call. She thanked me for making the trip all the way to come see her, and she was happy I wasn't like any of those guys who talk about coming to visit and yet never fulfill a promise. I told her I wasn't like that, and I couldn't wait to see what she looked underneath her clothes. That got her giggling in my ear; she too couldn't wait for us to meet.

The rest of the day went like a breeze. I went for a walk to the Market place to buy some stuff then returned to the motel later. There was a lot of older couples staying there, made the place seem like it was a joint waiting to be turned into a retirement home. I watched some TV, slept off and then woke up, walked around a bit, went out and got something to eat... anything to make the hour run fast. A good thing I tried to look at my watch less.

I got the call from the hubby sometime around 6:12p.m. He told me he'd just walked into the house and the wife will be arriving any minute and they'd both be over to visit me within the next hour. My blood was rushing like a bastard. Outside the sky gradually went dark.

The hour that was 7:00p.m., arrived. I got a call from the wife minutes later telling me they were on their way. I gave them my room number – Room 257.

I was looking out the window when I saw a maroon-coloured Buick drive into the motel compound. The wife and the hubby got out the car and almost immediately I recognized the wife from the numerous pictures the hubby had sent to me. I called them to let them know where my room was situated and waited for them to arrive. I heard the knock on my door and went and opened it and let them inside.

They'd come rather equipped for the evening: the hubby had a camera and tripod stand and a nylon bag full of Budweiser beer while the wife had a flask cup full of Barcardi. She looked hot wearing a black top and skirt. I sent the white boi hubby out to go get me some pack of gum so the wife and I could sit and talk for a few minutes. She seemed kind of nervous at first and I don't blame her for that – the first time of meeting is usually the nervous stage that needs to be gotten past. We sat next to each other on the bed and I got a sip of some of her Barcardi drink, although my eyes were peaking down at her ample cleavage. She had a large pair of tits, and when I undressed her top off, they just about fell out unto my hands; her nipples erect and waiting. I noticed too she had both a 'Queen of Spades' symbol and a 'Black Cock Slut' tattooed on each of her tits. I pulled at each of them before taking a bite off each. Her hubby returned some minutes later and I told him where to sit his ass down while Michelle and I got busy.

The light in the room was low; the TV volume on mute. I got to tasting Barcardi out the wife's lips as we tongue-kissed each other. Hubby got out his camera but waited till when I told him to start taking pictures. He loved the sight of Michelle and me playing with each other. I laid her down and pressed my face between her tits; I sucked on each one like a wild lion.

I was so hard inside my jeans. I called at the hubby to come over and help me undress her. Josh did as told, helping the wife out of her skirt and light-green panties; I hung that one around the white boi's neck and told him to wear it like a necktie for me, which he did. The wife was already gasping when I pushed her to lie back on the bed and let my tongue find the entrance to her pussy. She was somewhat hairy down there, and I cursed at the white boi for not having the courtesy to give her a shave, something which all hubbies ought to do for their wives without them asking. But I got down my knees and I ate that pussy like a real man ought to. At one time I told the hubby to pass me my Budweiser beer and I took a sip of it and held it in my mouth and soaked it over her pussy while still eating her; that got her wiggling like crazy.

Though it didn't last. She wanted the real black dick and wouldn't stop moaning for it.

I came and laid on my back on the bed and brought the slut over to come sit on my face, but not before I instructed the white boi to come undo the belt buckle of my jeans for her. He came over and did just that, freeing my black cock from its prison and offering the head to the wife. I felt her mouth start to suck on me and it got me eating her pussy even harder.

The white boi too got out of his clothes – his wife ordered him to – and made him kneel before me and ordered him to open his mouth and get a taste of my cock. He seemed to enjoy himself while he did it. The wife got jealous and pushed him aside and took control of my cock once more, all the time moaning about how she just loves the taste of black cock. I told hubby to search inside my bag and he took out a dog leash and I tied it around the slut's neck and made her to keep worshiping my dick. She then looked like a 'Black-Owned' slut.

Her man went and got his camera and that was when I gave him permission to take some pictures.

***

I got the slut down from the bed and with the leash around her neck was pulling her around the room with her mouth stuck on my dick. She had a thick lock of brunette hair and I kept pushing it off her face because I loved watching those lips of hers being buried around my dick; she looked totally beautiful that way. All the time I kept talking to her, asking her how she loved that dick … what she'd want that black cock to do to her … how sexy and beautiful she looked. I called out at the white boi and asked if he too agreed with me on that. He too nodded his head and replied how she'd talked only about wanting my cock in her mouth and her pussy and ass and nothing more. To hear him talk like that got my dick hard even more, and I knew he too wanted a taste of it.

"Hey white boi, how about you drop that camera down and come share this dick as well!" I ordered him.

He slung his camera around his neck and came and knelt beside his wife and the both of them worshipped my cock like it was the best thing they've had. I'd take my shaft in my hand and slap it against their faces, rubbing their saliva over their cheeks and just watching them fight of that black stick. It was so amusing too hearing the wife snap at the hubby whenever he'd gotten too much taste and grabbed my dick it back from him. She grazed her teeth against my nuts and though it kind of hurt … it felt damn good too!

The white boi sat back on the floor while I got the wife back on the bed. She got on her arms and knees, bent forward with that thick juicy white ass of hers sticking up my face, looking like the world's most expensive Cadillac. I shit you not! I sunk a finger into her pussy while I pressed my tongue into her anal hole. Seconds later I added a second finger and rubbed at her clit while my tongue kept fucking her ass. The bitch was moaning like crazy, groaning about wanting the dick. She had a thick labia and it tasted soft and sweet between my lips when i pulled at it. Her hubby was down between my legs tugging at my cock; I gave the white boi some leg room and allowed him to get some licks in while I kept tongue-fucking the wife's ass.

I climbed to my feet and rubbed the head of my cock against the wife's pussy entrance before thrusting it inside. Her pussy felt real warm and cold at the same time. But it felt genuinely good too, like shoving your dick between the comfort of a pillow. I took a moment to enjoy the warmth, letting her pussy tighten around my shaft before pulling back and then shoving it back in again. I was all excitement and my heart was beating like an African drum inside my chest while the slut brought her thick ass back at me.

"Slap my ass!" she cried out with her head bent forward on the bed. "Go ahead, slap my butt!"

She didn't have to tell me that because I was already slapping those ass cheeks while slamming against her. Her hubby came and stood beside me, watching. He took a couple snapshots before dropping down his camera; he didn't want to miss sight of the action taking place. He too urged me to fuck the bitch harder ... give her some of that hard black cock ... it's what she's here for, it's what she's been begging for all day. The hubby still had her panties around his neck. He took it down and wrapped it around his cock and went on stroking as he watched.

The sound of her butt hitting against my lower abdomen ... my hands slapping her butt each turn ... her hubby coming to stand in front of her and letting her to pull at his cock while she was getting fucked from behind ... it all added magic to the room. I grabbed at the leash on her neck and pulled her head back off from the bed. I smacked her butt even harder and that got her rejuvenated. I tried to get up on the bed to fuck her from above, but the thickness of her ass wouldn't enable me; nearly made me fall on my backside.

I pulled out of her, not wanting to cum right away, and to my surprise noticed I wasn't getting hard anymore.

"Yo, white boi! Better get your ass over here and do your job," I said to Josh.

I laid on the bed and the wife slumped down on her face, gasping. Both of us breathed against each other's face. She crawled half on top of me and we kissed with passion while her hubby came and knelt on the bed's edge and resumed stroking and sucking my cock back to full erection. The wife grabbed at his head and kept pushing him down on me, snapping at him to go ahead and get that black cock hard for her again. The white boi sure knew how to deep-throat a back cock, I'll tell you that. Between the both of them I could hardly tell who sucked cock the best. So enthusiastic was he and she added vigor to her own mouth works when she slid down to join him. I pulled the slut back up and sucked on her heavy pair of tits which hung over my face; her hand slipped between my kegs and stroked my cock for her hubby who was still hard at work getting me hard; the white boi succeeded at that immensely.

The slut wife, Michelle, climbed on top of me; her thick hair fell over my face and I kept having to push it back to her shoulder while she sat down on me. It was hard getting my dick between those ass cheeks of hers and her hubby was there to lend a hand, grabbing my cock and thrusting it into her wet pussy.

"Go ahead, babe," I heard the white boi talk to the wife. "Go ahead, ride that black dick!"

She was groaning and grunting at the same time while that ass rode me. I could barely get my arms around her to get a good hold on her ass cheeks; I couldn't stop slapping her butt. I love it when a woman rides me, and were it not for her hair tickling my face, I probably would have cum right there and then. My dick kept slipping out of her – her pussy was so wet from all the excitement going on in the room and we were both sweating from everything.

She came off me and we opted to take a break. Her hubby handed her the flask of Barcadi in it and gave me back my can of Budweiser. We got to talking while we sipped our drinks. They asked of how recent it was that I came into the country, and of how I got my sexual adventures started along with my blog. The wife, Michelle, was most upset that all the time the hubby and I had been communicating back when I was in Nigeria that I never once bothered to speak with her on the phone. I told her I wanted to make that my surprise. Also, I didn't want them to think I wasn't going to keep my promise in the end of coming to the U.S., to come and see them. I'm not all that good at keeping promises, but when I do make one, it's hard for me not to keep it. She told me about her place of work: how some of her white colleagues have on numerous times tried to talk her into having sex with them but being a good slut, she'd always turned them down, not wanting to get anything to do with any dick not unless its black. The hubby too supports her in this and told me of how long its been since last time she had a taste of black cock and that when she heard I was in country she'd been itching for me to travel down their way.

The slut's hubby popped me another beer and the wife and I shared this one. I poured some of the alcohol down her neckline, watched it run like a river down her bosom. My brought my face closer and licked it off her flesh and went back to sucking on her breasts. Her man came over and sucked on her other pair of breasts. The wife allowed him for a while then pushed him off to go back to reviving my dick back, which he did. The wife and I fucked once more. My only regret was I couldn't stay hard enough to fuck her asshole; she was definitely in need of that one. I allowed her and her hubby to fuck for a while, and took the camera and took snapshots of them (although I got to delete them later). Another time the wife climbed on top of me and the hubby came at her ass.

I couldn't believe the time was running all this while. To tell the truth, it felt as if the night had stopped moving. The curtains were drawn closed but it was transparent enough to make out the day, and all that was behind it was darkness. Michelle wouldn't stop hollering and for a moment I got scared that the sound of her cries was going to wake up any of my neighbours at the motel and have them go complain to the staff about the noise coming out of Room 257. At the same time I hopped they'd hear, and maybe the couples close by would get to fucking too knowing that some hard fucking was going on in the room next to theirs. Sounds wicked, but that was what I had in mind.

At one time I turned the bitch over to be on her side, held one of her legs over my shoulder and just sunk my dick all the way between those folds of flesh to get at her pussy; her hubby came by her side and she accepted his dick. A while later when I'd cummed inside her, hubby came to eat her pussy while I fed her my dick. The slut rubbed her tongue down my balls and back.

Minutes later to my surprise, I felt like cumming again.

I lay on the bed next to the bitch and the hubby came to suck my cock, rolling his mouth and tongue down my shaft, deep-throating it back and forth, then rolling his tongue and lips around my bullet-head of my dick. The white boi was sucking it so damn hard, and I was gasping from it. The moment came and I pushed the white boi off and climbed on top of the wife's chest and stroked my cock hard enough till I shot my load over her tits and chin. I was shaking all over while this happened and it took some effort for me to get off the wife. When I did, I grabbed the white boi's head and ordered him to come do what he ought to do. The white boi knew it too and came to the wife's aid to clean.

"Go ahead, white boi," it was her turn to give him orders. "Clean your slut wife."

The white boi gobbled up my cum from her tits like ice cream. He slid on top her and licked off the droplets on her chin and when he was done, shared some of it with her.

"Don't forget me too, white boi!" said I.

I came forward with my cock still dripping cum and my shaft wet with the wife's pussy juice. I made them kneel before me once again and they got to sharing my cock again. I told them to do it good; they got the message and did just that.

***

It was past 1:15a.m., when they decided to take their leave. The hubby helped the wife dress up, left the beer for me and took his camera as well. I put on my clothes and walked with them out to where they'd parked their ride. They wife and I went on kissing while the hubby stowed things away. He took some snapshots of us; he loved the way we stood next to each other kissing. It was unfortunate I was leaving the following day, though I promised to return in the near future. And next time, it's not going to end in just one night!

We waved at each other as they reversed out of the driveway back onto the road and drove off into the night. My erection came knocking back in my pants.

***

A week has passed since I last got a taste of my hot slut in Rochester, NY. Yes, I'm right now seated here in my apartment typing these words on my laptop while taking turns to admire the snapshots we'd taken that fateful night at the Super 8 motel. The slut has sent me a couple new ones she took just for me, and they've got me hard just looking at them. Matter of fact, it's almost like gazing at the sun; there's no way I can admire her pictures of her sexy body without my dick kicking its head inside my jeans.

You don't get to fuck a pussy like that and then think of it as a one-night stand. There's a thing that comes with fucking a hot milf: a hot wife who knows what she wants … and that she's got herself a cuck hubby who really is in understanding with her and too wants to be dominated by a black bull. Such type of luck don't always fall down from the sky. And when they do fall, you're never there to watch it happen.

There's plenty of white bois out there who want the same thing too. Sure, they huff and puff and try not to let it bother them… that's like going to the beach but never letting your feet get wet by the water. There's a lot of white bois out there who wish they too have got a hot wife like this one: a sexy slut who'd be a great lover for black men wherever and whenever she can get her hands on them, and who would humiliate her white boi hubbies to get them to do whatever's necessary that she gets her satisfaction. Oh yes, that's the word: satisfaction. For the wife, its about getting that black cock swimming inside her pussy and ass … making sure that black cock gets to fill every nook and cranny of her wet hole. That the bull is man enough to use her like the piece of bitch-slut that she is, and even when she thinks the fucking has ended, the bull pulls up her face and slaps her cheek with his dick and snaps at her to open up.

And what about the hubby? Let's not go on and forget about him. A cuckold circle can't ever be complete if the hubby isn't in there to catch a feel of what's going on. Don't matter if the hubby/boyfriend just wants to lie on the next bed and watch, wants to join in … no matter what of it, the hubby too gets to see up-close what the wife has been dying to have for a long time. And if the hubby is lucky, he too will be rewarded by that essence which he's always craved for: some sloppy seconds from the wife.

Nothing is more rewarding that when a hubby gets to eat out his slut wife's pussy. Just the sight of seeing that swollen pussy that once he thought was his but isn't any longer gets him excited and throbbing like excitement all through. Even better when the hubby comes to the Black bull's aid, caressing his balls, cheering the wife on, and even pushing her ass back each time the bull slams his dick into that hot pussy.

But the end of the result is quite clear for a lot of hubbies, wives and white couples out there: the dream of watching the wife's belly months later swell with obvious pregnancy. And both of them knowing it was the Black bull that was responsible for it!

I do still keep in touch with my owned couple in Rochester. Only a matter of time before I return to them once again and own and use that slut wife's pussy once again. Even now she's calling my phone wanting to know when.

The Best Friend

Joe parked his car not too far from the house; it was late in the evening and the street was dark and empty. Just the way he wanted it to be, he smiled to himself as he got out of the car, slammed the door and approached the designated house. He stood at the garden hedge from where he had a good view of the front yard. The living room lights were on, but Joe knew only the woman was inside—her husband wasn't around. Joe knew this because he had done his work thoroughly before deciding tonight to make his move. He didn't need to wear a mask. His black shirt and pants matched with his dark skin; he would be in and out before anyone even knew he was here.

He went through a narrow walkway beside the garden hedge that led in the direction of the backyard. He stopped when he got there, saw the kitchen light was on through the back window and smiled when he saw the man's wife—or rather, his fiancée—doing the dishes. This was going to be even easier than he thought, he smiled and licked his lips. He approached the back door carefully on a pair of light feet and eased the handle carefully. The woman was humming a song to herself, her back towards him as she took the washed dishes and was placing them inside a cupboard high above her head. Joe entered the kitchen and leaving the door slightly ajar, rushed towards her.

Kate was caught in her humming and jumping like someone who'd just been goosed as she felt a pair of hands cover her face from behind. She felt like screaming but the same pair of hands were upon her mouth as well. The plate she had in her hands nearly fell from her fingers, but they didn't. She inhaled the intruder's breath as he rescued the plate from her hand at the same time turned her around.

"Are you alone, bitch?" he whispered the question to her; there was menace in his voice.

She wanted to speak but what escaped her lips was a muffled groan. Instead she nodded her head that she indeed was alone.

"Good. I don't want to hurt you, but I want you to do exactly what I want you to do, bitch. If you dare try anything funny, I'm going to snap your neck. You hear me?"

Again she shook her head; she was shaking like a leaf.

Joe led her out of the kitchen and into the house. They went into the living room and he went and drew the blinds of the front windows closed before turning to face her. Kate was wearing an evening dress like she'd had plans of going out for the evening when actually she didn't. What scared her most was that Elliot, her soon-to-be husband was out of town; she was stuck in her home with a psycho and no one to come to her rescue.

The black man gripped her arm behind her back and pushed down her left sleeve of her dress, presenting him with one naked pair of tit. His hand grasped it and she flinched even as he was caressing her flesh. He fingered her nipple which in turn responded to his touch. Kate tried to fight him, her first thought being that the man was about to rape her. Joe brought his face to her chest and pressed his mouth of her breasts. Kate was still fighting and struggling to be free, crying out but at the same time groaning from the ministrations of his mouth. The black man pushed down the other sleeve off her arm, practically ripping her dress off her and attacked her other pair of tit too. His hands were all over her, groping and caressing and gripping her body while at the same time he pressed her body against his. This was torture for Kate and there was nothing she could do about it. The black man pushed her down to her knees and slapped her cheek, enforcing his menace on her. One hand gripped her throat while his other hand worked his belt buckle and then his zipper. His hand reached inside the slit of his jeans and rummaged inside before whipping out a thick black snake unlike anything Kate had seen before. She cried out and fought to be free but the black man gripped her hair and pushed her face against his crotch, yelling at her at the same time.

"The fuck are you running off to, bitch!" he bent her over, pulled up her dress to reveal her thong panties and her buttocks. Kate cried out when he gave her ass cheeks double smacks. "Don't you ever fucking try that again, you hear me, you fucking slut! Now get over here and suck this dick! Open that pretty mouth of yours and suck it!"

He thrust his cock at her face and this time Kate didn't pretend to fight. She accepted his cock and let him slip the round black head into her mouth. She had never held a black cock before, never even been out with a black man in all her twenty-three years … and now here she was, being forced on her knees by a cruel black man and taking his prick in her mouth. Joe kept choking her face with his cock. He held her face and fucked her mouth back and forth while long threads of saliva dribbled down the side of her mouth. Kate couldn't stop grunting from the hurt she was undergoing. Joe held up his shaft and ordered her to go ahead and suck his balls, which she did. By this time Kate was sucking his cock like her life depended on it.

"Alright, that's fucking enough, bitch!"

Joe picked her up from the floor and pushed her towards one of the couch seats. He made her lean over it, pushed up the back of her dress and before Kate could utter a protest, he pushed the underside of her thong panties to the side and spat down on the head of his cock before thrusting it between her pussy slit. Kate cried from the sharp pain and she gripped the couch's fabric and Joe went on tearing his way into her. He slapped her ass cheeks periodically while he kept fucking her from behind. Kate was moaning now and grunting from the slamming he was meting on her, not giving her any chance to recover. Sometime later Joe pulled out of her but told her to remain as she was while he hurriedly undressed. Finished, he came back and drove his cock back into her cunt. He grabbed a fistful of her long brown her and pulled her face backward till she was almost staring back at him. He leaned against her and licked the side of her neck. His breathing was frantic as compared to hers. His hand reached for her breasts and she howled as he pinched and pulled at one of her nipple.

He gave her buttocks one last slap before pulling out of her. Kate rested against the couch, trying to catch her breath, but her moment of reprieve lasted only a few seconds as Joe pulled her away from the couch. She fell on her backside and nearly fell on the centre table. Joe came and pushed the centre table away, as Kate lay there on the floor with her legs sticking up in the air. He told her to remain as she was as he came and crouched over her, pushed her panties to the side and thrust his cock downward on her pussy. Kate by now was in the zone. She held her legs backward and watched with numbing shock at the way the black man's cock went sliding downward and then out of her cunt. Joe fucked her steadily like this for a while then turned around, facing the couch and leaning down on it while his cock searched for Kate's pussy. She reached up for it and tucked it down into her waiting hole and like that Joe resumed pounding her pussy.

Minutes later he turned around once up and picked Kate up from the floor. He removed the remainder of her now torn dress from her and lifted her up in the air. Kate's leg instinctively came around his waistline. Joe's shaft beat against her buttocks; this time it was Kate who slipped his cock inside her hungry hole. Grabbing her ass, he was slamming into her before she even had time to catch her breath, crying so loud she thought she could feel the head of his cock hitting against her chest. Joe was gasping heavily and had to stop to lower Kate back down to her feet. She staggered somewhat and Joe caught her arm before she could slip. Lifting her in his arms like she was his bride, he took her upstairs to where the bedroom was.

Unknown to Kate, her husband Elliot hadn't actually travelled at all. All the time Joe had been fucking his fiancée, he'd positioned himself outside the front doorway holding a video camera to his eye. Joe had drawn the curtains closed, but not all the way close. There was just enough space for his camera's eye to film the action that was taking place inside his home. He was breathing through his mouth as he filmed his black friend fuck his soon-to-be bride. He watched as Joe picked Kate up and then disappeared out of the room. He knew where they were going and he too wanted to be up there with them.

Elliot took off and ran down the hedge path to the back of the house. He entered through the kitchen and went through the narrow passageway to the stairs and with his camera still filming, he went up the stairs two at a time. Even before he got to the door he could hear sounds of giggles and moaning coming from behind it. He opened the door and entered the bedroom.

Kate sat on the bed while Joe stood beside her and she was busy stroking his cock at the same time rolling it around her mouth when she turned and saw Elliot standing there by the bed smiling at her with the video camera in his free hand. He waved at her.

"Hiya, babe," said Elliot, "smile for the camera!"

Kate couldn't help but laugh. "My God, Elliot! I thought it was going to be just me and Joe."

"Sorry, darling, I just had to watch you and get some of it on tape. Go on with what you're doing, you're doing a good job already."

Kate resumed taking her husband's friend's cock into her mouth, her hands held his thighs as she made herself deep-throat his cock and then pulled out of him, gasping. Joe held the underside of her jaw and slapped his cock against her open mouth before tucking it back inside.

Elliot placed the video camera on a tripod stand beside the bed and aimed the camera at them while he began taking off his clothes. Soon he stood there naked, stroking his cock while he continued directing them. By this time, Joe now was lying on the bed and Kate was riding him. She leaned forward over him. Joe raised his thighs and was pounding his fiancé's pussy hard, making the bed quake. Elliot took the camera off the tripod and stood by the head of the bed and watched the way Kate rolled her buttocks over his friend's black cock, the way her pussy swallowed his dick, milking it, really drove him crazy. Joe slapped her ass cheeks, spurring her to grind her ass harder. Joe turned her over on the bed now on top of her and kept on pounding her harder. Kate had already climaxed and the more Joe went on sinking his cock inside her she knew it wasn't long before she climaxed once again. He sunk his hands down under her buttocks and kept pounding her pussy.

"Hey, bitch!" Joe grunted at her face. "Whose fucking pussy is this?"

Kate who now had her arms and legs locked around his body, moaning like crazy, answered: "Yours! It's yours ... it's your pussy!"

"Yeah, it's my fucking pussy! And don't you ever forget it, bitch! You're getting married to my friend, but your pussy belongs to me, you hear?"

"Awwwwhhh ... yes! Yes, Joe! Fuck me ... make me fucking cum!"

Joe did as she wanted and worked his thighs between her legs. His cock soaked between her juice which was flowing out of her cunt and staining the sheets. Kate felt her body spasm uncontrollably and she held onto her black lover tight and pressed herself against him as she felt her body quake against his. Joe too grounded himself down on her and sunk his cock all the way down to his balls and he too groaned as he filled her pussy with his cum.

Elliot came up on the bed and filmed his friend's cum seeping out of his woman's pussy. Joe pulled out of her and rolled off to the other side of the bed, his cock dragging some of her cum with him. Elliot zoomed his camera's eye on his wife's cum-filled pussy, grinning.

"Yeah, that's a swelled-up pussy, alright," he muttered. "You did good, babe."

Kate smiled at him. "If you think so, then how about you come down here and lick his cum off me."

Elliot turned off the camera and dropped it and then grabbed his soon-to-be wife's thighs and pulled her cunt towards his face and began licking his tongue between her pussy's lips.

***

Later that night, Joe lay sleeping on a mattress beside the bed when he swore he was hearing sounds coming from on top the bed. Not only that, the bed too was shaking. He slapped his hand around the side of his pillow for his luminous wristwatch and found it and looked at the time. It was 02:36 a.m. There came the familiar voice of Kate issuing off a lengthy moan; no doubt Joe was getting at her once again. Elliot scrambled to his feet and searched for the table lamp beside the bed and turned it on.

Bright light flooded the room and there was Joe with his head stuck between Kate's legs which were beating a steady percussion on the bed. Elliot went for his video camera. He switched the lamp's light off and filmed the two of them together in the dark. Joe got up and came to Kate's side and he muttered a groan as she wrapped her hand around his cock followed by her mouth. Elliot was smiling to himself as he captured them moment on film. He hovered from side to side of the bed, and then an idea came to him. He got the camera's tripod stand and reduced its legs and planted the camera on it. He set it to be filming his best friend with his fiancé together while he went looking inside a drawer and found what he was looking for—his digital camera. He stood away from the filming camera's path and took snapshots of both of them. Kate turned towards him and cracked a smile.

"Is this what you've always wanted, honey?" she said to him.

"Oh yes, babe. I've always loved seeing you like this." He took another quick successive snapshot of her sucking on his friend's cock. He sucked air through his teeth while he watched them, going around from one angle to another. "My God, Kate, you're so fucking sexy."

"Damn fine woman she is," Joe crooned while he hand grabbed her hair and she muttered grunting fits as he thrust his cock further and further into her mouth. He leaned to the side and fingered her pussy. "Such a fine cunt you've got here. You can marry your man here whenever you want, but this pussy's mine."

"Uh-Huh," she muttered while her mouth still choked on his prick.

He retrieved his cock and came off her and pushed her to lie backward, her legs open before him. Joe came between them and Kate held onto him and both of them groaned as his cock slid into her wet hole. Elliot lowered his head and took snapshots of the back of his friend's buttocks, catching sight of his cock sinking all the way into his fiancée's cunt. Within seconds her cries were echoing and rebounding around the room as Joe dug his thighs down on the bed and his buttocks bounced up and down on her. Elliot watched his cock half pull out and then slammed back into his woman's cum-dripping pussy like a machine. Kate went into convulsive shakes and her legs rose high above her lover's backside. Joe dug his hands under her butt cheeks and cupped them hard and went on pounding her pussy, fucking her down into the bed, punishing her with his prick. He half stood up and holding her arms kept on ramming her hard. Kate was gulping her breaths like staccato blasts. Joe fell backward, pulling her along.

Kate came forward and balanced herself on top of him. Elliot carried the camera from where it stood and went to the other side of the bed to film his fiancée's buttocks riding and bouncing against his friend's thighs. He took snapshots of his cock pushing up into her cunt from behind. He grasped her ass cheeks and gave it a gentle slap while she went on crying on top his friend's cock. She moaned uncontrollable as her pussy spasmed on top of him; Joe slapped her ass and told her to keep riding him. Kate was on the throes of climaxing and just as the pressure built up in her, she exploded with unbridled lust over his cock. Joe too came not long after she did, blowing his wad of cum inside her. Kate fell forward over him, feeling his cum run down her pussy, staining the bed sheets.

Elliot took snapshots of his friend's white semen pouring out of his wife's cunt. He licked his lips and suddenly a moment of epiphany came upon him. He dropped his camera and spread Kate's ass cheeks wide enough and licked his tongue up and down her ass crack, downward to taste the saltiness of his friend's cum. He flicked his tongue between the folds of Kate's pussy, sucked on her cum juice together with his friend's sperm load. Kate muttered a sigh and her pussy seemed to twitch at the feel of her fiancé's tongue perusing and licking through her. Elliot's tongue brushed over his friend's cock and he couldn't help himself as he picked up his cock and took it into his mouth and sucked him off, feeling his cock spurt tiny drops of semen into his mouth. Done with sucking him, he went on cleaning both of them and didn't stop till he licked off every drop.

When he was done, he left them to cuddle with each other and returned to his bed by the floor. He ran his tongue over his lips. The taste of his friend's cock resonated in his mouth, so too his semen and Kate's cum juice. He regretted he hadn't left the light on. He would love to take a snapshot of himself in that position someday.

***

The following morning the three of them awoke looking tired and groggy yet happy with each other. Joe went into the bathroom to shower and when he came out began putting on his clothes saying he needed to rush home and change or else he'd be late for work. Elliot and Kate said goodbye to him; she promised giving him a call later in the day.

After they'd showered they went downstairs for Kate to fix both of them breakfast. Elliot still had an hour to burn before he went off to work as a software programmer for a data-managing company. Kate was still working on acquiring her Master's degree at the U and wasn't yet ready to finding herself a job. Besides, the income Elliot was making was enough for them to start up a home for themselves. They'd known each other since college and had fallen in love and remained tight with each other all through graduation. Elliot and Kate had known Joe back in college as well. He'd been a varsity player for the college football team and would have gone pro had he wanted to, but instead he'd opted for knowledge rather than getting hit and slammed upon on the field. Their friendship had remained steady even as they left and had taken an intimate turn the moment Elliot had suggested to his friend that he fuck his wife-to-be.

As they sat at the kitchen table eating their breakfast, Kate dressed in her pink robe while Elliot wore a shirt and tie, he narrated to her what he'd done last night while he'd cleaned her pussy of his friend's cum. Kate looked at him incredulously while she stirred her cup of tea and then took a sip of it.

"You really did it?" she asked with amazement in her voice. "You actually sucked his cock?"

"Yes, I did."

Elliot thought she was going to reach across and slap his face for ever doing such a dirty thing but instead Kate drew his face towards hers and kissed him.

"That's incredible, darling," she said. "I'm still surprised that you actually did it. Or was it because the light was off?"

He shrugged. "I don't know. The feeling just came to me. I know you've always wanted me to kind of do it and I've been putting it off lots of times. Last night, I guess I was just in the mood for it."

"I wonder how Joe must have felt about it," she said to him.

"He didn't seem to mind … or did hc, do you think?"

Kate shook her head. "He would have reacted if he did, but I doubt it. He probably has been wanting you to do such before now."

"I'll probably ask him to have lunch with me later so we can talk about it. I feel kind of nervous that I surprised him the way I did."

"Stop sounding like that, honey. This is Joe we're talking about. He's as much a friend to you as he is to me. Give him a call and have lunch with him if you like. Get it off your chest then."

"Yeah, that's exactly what I'll do. But you were fucking amazing last night."

She smiled at him. "Thanks. Joe has got a beautiful cock, and every time he's fucking me, I swear sparks shoot out of my pussy."

Elliot laughed. "I'll bet. A good thing I've got them on video. I'd better be off now. I'll talk to you later." He finished his tea and they shared a kiss before he took his leave.

***

Later that morning when he had a few minutes free from his office's workload, Elliot went downstairs towards the direction of the men's room in the building his office was located at and dialled his friend's number. The line got picked up after the second ring and Joe's familiar voice said hello to him.

"Hey there, Joe. Kate wanted me to tell you she had a swell time last night," he said.

"She's so sweet to say that."

"Yeah, she is, really. Anyway, I was wondering if you and I can have lunch together. I've some stuff I'd like to air out with you."

"Sure, no problem. You got any spot in mind?"

"How about we meet at Sprago's. It's not that far from where you work."

"Okay, no problem. I'll get off at noon and I'll head down there and meet you."

"That's good. I'll see you there."

They hung up at each other. Elliot pocketed his phone and returned to his office.

Noon came and a quarter past the hour, Elliot took off towards the direction of the restaurant he'd told his friend to meet with him. He was there early as he didn't spot his friend around when he stepped inside, away from the hot autumn sun. He got himself a table and ordered an espresso while he waited. Joe showed up nearly fifteen minutes later; his office building was less than two blocks from the restaurant. He wore his shirt and tie and his shirt sleeves were folded up to his elbows. I waved at him and he came over and shook hands before taking our seat. He made our order and did idle talk after the waitress had gone to fetch our meal. I took my time to measure my words before I said anything.

"Joe, there's something I want to talk to you about," he hesitated while Joe sat there waiting for me to continue. "It's about what … what I did last night." I lowered my voice as I got to this part.

"Okay," he said with a neutral voice.

"After you'd fucked Kate," Elliot said in a tight, low voice. "When I sucked your cock…"

He nodded as if he'd expected this was what I'd wanted to see him about, though his eyes remained expressionless as I stumbled on.

"It wasn't something I wanted to do. I was even surprised that I did it."

Joe shrugged. "But you did it. So why the worried look?"

"I figured you'd kind of be mad I did it," he said carefully.

"Do I look like I'm mad about it?"

Elliot looked at his friend earnestly, surprised by his calm demeanour. "What? You really weren't upset about it, none at all?"

"Upset? Nah! I liked it, really. I was even going to make you do it to me one of these days if you hadn't made the move first."

Elliot fell back on his chair relieved by what he'd just heard. "Oh man, I never knew. And here I was, thinking you'd be seriously pissed about what I'd done."

"Look, it's fun you did it. You and I have been friends long enough, so I know last night wasn't some gay episode of yours. Don't sweat it. Matter of fact, I'd like you to do it next time I drop by."

Elliot had to smile this time. "Kate would go crazy about that. I know she'd like to see me do it."

"Give her a call when you get back to your desk and tell her about it and hear what she has to say."

"Trust me I'll do that as soon as I get back there," Elliot nodded with excitement tingling through his nerves.

Their food arrived and they talked about other stuff while they ate.

An hour later, Elliot was back at his office building. Before going upstairs, he went in the direction of the men's room and dialled his fiancée's cell phone. She answered the phone on its second ring.

"Hello, darling," she murmured into the mouthpiece.

"Hi, honey," Elliot spoke into her ear. "How's your afternoon going?"

"Same old, same old. I just got back from the library and I'm fixing myself a hot bath right now when you called."

"That's good to hear. Joe and I talked about what happened last night, and he says he's okay about it."

"Yes, I know."

Elliot stopped. "You know? How could you know about it already?"

The sound of her voice laughing into his ear. "Joe and I spoke some minutes ago, that's how I know. He's looking forward to us having another romp soon. He says that this time, he's going to make you suck his cock all the way," she crackled. "He told me that he's going to turn you into his bitch!"

Elliot couldn't believe he'd heard her right. He turned around to make sure he was still alone then spoke tightly into the phone. "He'd turn me into his bitch. Were those his exact words?"

"Uh-Huh! And he said more. Do you want to know more of what he said?"

His cock nodded its head inside his pants. Elliot felt it and turned to face the wall when he observed two of his company workers laughing as they strolled into the men's room. Elliot looked like one running a fever. He couldn't believe the words his fiancée had just told him coming from his friend whom he'd had lunch with less than a half hour ago. It's no wonder he told me to call Kate once I returned to the office. He'd never been this excited before.

"Elliot, are you still there?"

"Yes, yes, babe, I'm still here. I'm just soaking in what you said Joe mentioned to you."

She laughed again. "Wait till you hear what else he told me. He said he'd like to watch me force your head down on him. Wants to see me spank your ass and make you suck his cock like the white boi he says that you are." She burst into laughter some more.

The door of the men's room opened again and Elliot covered the phone's mouthpiece with his hand and muttered 'hello', at the guys as they shuffled past him. When they were gone, he returned the phone to his ear.

"Babe, did he … did he really say that?" he just about whispered the question.

"Yes, he did, honey. He said a lot more though. I'll bet you're just itching to hear what else that is."

Elliot thought he could hear himself moan. "Please, tell me. Please, darling."

"Hmmm … no, I won't now. I'll tell you about it once you return home. Go back to work, honey. I'll see you when you're here."

They said goodbyes and I-love-you to each other before hanging up. Elliot went into the men's room and checked underneath the stalls. Glad that the place was empty for now, he entered one of the stalls, quickly pulled down his pants and frced his cock from inside her jockey briefs and proceeded to jerk off. It was a most satisfying one.

***

Elliot drove home with a vengeance. He almost scraped against a fleeting Hummer truck and was lucky there wasn't a cop in sight as he cruised towards home, towards where Kate was waiting for him. He had a rampaging hard-on inside his pants. All the time he'd returned to his work station he could barely concentrate much; his mind kept replying the words his fiancée had mentioned to him of what his friend had told her. The picture that coalesced in his mind was one he couldn't shake out of, not to mention the excitement that came with it.

He sped into his street and didn't pull on the break until he came fifteen feet of the front door to his home. He left everything else inside the car as he got out and ran towards the front door as if the house itself was on fire. He yelled out Kate's name as he slammed the door close behind him.

"Up here, honey!" her voice hollered at him.

Her voice came from the bedroom upstairs. He took the stairs two at a time and stopped at the top landing to catch his breath. The bedroom door creaked open and Joe appeared by the doorway naked with his cock hanging downward between his legs, glistening wet with cum juice. He took a swig off a Heineken beer he had in his hand; his eyes gloated at his friend's presence. From inside the bedroom, hidden from his view, Elliot heard the unmistakable moans that could only be Kate's voice.

"Good of you to hurry back home, white boi," Joe muttered a belch. "How about you strip right now and crawl your ass in here."

Elliot found his hands going to his neck and loosening his tie and shirt buttons. He threw every item of clothes from his body while Joe leaned against the door watching him and drinking his beer. Elliot soon stood before him in just his pair of briefs and shoe stockings; his erection stood at attention inside his briefs. Joe indicated for him to fall to his knees. Elliot did as his friend wanted and came down on all fours and crawled as directed into the bedroom he shared with his soon-to-be wife, Kate while Joe closed the door behind him.

"Hey, Kate, look at who just crawled in," laughed Joe.

Kate was on the bed with her legs flung apart fucking her cunt with a black dildo, moaning from the exchange. When she heard her lover call out her name, she stopped what she was doing and looked at his direction. Her eyes found her darling Elliot crawling towards the bed and almost immediately she shook with laughter.

"Oh my God, Elliot!" she sniggered. "You're looking so pathetic right now."

"He is indeed," Joe indicated for Elliot to stop. "Look at the white boi's boner. I can't believe this is what you want fucking you after you both get married."

"Oh, I doubt Elliot will be fucking me ever all at," she purred. "Not with you around to take care of my pussy for me."

"That's good for you to say so, and don't forget it either. This white pussy you've got is off limits to this white boi here." Joe drained the rest of his beer and taking his cock in his hand approached Elliot and started waving it inches from his face.

"Here you go, white boi," he taunted him. "You been thinking about this black cock, haven't you. Answer me!"

"Yes … yes, sir, I have," Elliot answered, mesmerised by the swinging cock. His mouth hung open and he licked his tongue back and forth over it.

"I can't tell you how much I enjoy fucking your slut's pussy. A good thing she's now my slut and not yours anymore. Here, why don't you try catching my cock with your mouth, see if you can taste her cum off my dick!"

Elliot opened his mouth wider and leaned his face forward, trying to catch his friend's black prick which danced and waved before his eyes like a restless swing. Kate came down from the bed, wearing just her bra and garter belt and hugged her lover while at the same time laughing at her fiancé's submissive position.

Elliot eventually caught Joe's black cock with his mouth and began sucking him. He wanted to bring up his hands to stroke him but Joe swatted his hands away and instructed him to use only his mouth. Now with both hands behind his backside, Elliot went on sucking his Master's prick. Tears rolled down the sides of his eyes and he grunted repeatedly as Joe kept on thrusting his prick in and out of his friend's face.

"Dammit, white boi," Joe growled impatiently. "Even a girl sucks a lollipop better than you. Kate, how about you giving white boi here a lending hand and show him how it's done."

"With pleasure," she said.

Kate slid down to her knees and took her lover's shaft from her fiancé's mouth and ingested it. Her mouth rolled back and forth over Joe's velvet-skinned prick like one putting on a hand glove while her hands below tugged at his balls. Joe too couldn't help but respond from the sucking episode she was giving him. He hands grabbed the sides of her head and started making periodic thrusts in and out of her mouth. Saliva flew from her mouth but Kate was undaunted. She stroked her Master's cock and licked her tongue up and down his cock's underside before once again taking this prick down her throat.

"Awww … yeah!" Joe whimpered. "Hope you're taking lessons from this, white boi. This is how a slut bitch is meant to blow a black man. Later you're going to start practising with that dildo of Kate's. Or maybe we'll get you one for yourself personally. You'd like that, wouldn't you, white boi?"

"Yes, Master, sir," Elliot looked up at him with deference in his eyes. "I'd really love that."

Kate handed her lover's cock back to Elliot and he absorbed lessons from her and immediately adapted his blow-job skills just like hers. Joe seemed to approve of this. He stepped backward and sat on the bed and watched as the couple feasted on his erect missile prick. They took turned sucking on his shaft and pulling at his balls, neither of them giving his cock a chance to escape from their clutch. Joe couldn't hold back much longer. He was getting closer towards cumming and both Elliot and Kate sensed this about to happen. Joe snatched his shaft from their grasp and began stroking it. The couple drew their face closer with their mouths open to receive.

"*I'M CUMMING … OHH SHIT! AAAHHHHGGGHHH … AAHHHH … AGGGHHHH!*"

Joe groaned while his hand pumped furiously at his cock and within seconds a spurt of semen shot out of his penis like a projectile and splattered over Kate's face. Elliot licked the cum off his fiancée's forehead while she brought her mouth to her Master's cock and kept sucking at every cum drop he let go of. Joe fell back on the bed totally spent while Kate and Elliot went on fighting over his cock which was gradually becoming flaccid. Kate kissed her fiancé, letting some of her lover's cum sip into his mouth and prodded him to swallow it. For that, Elliot didn't require much prodding at all.

Joe slid up on the bed and within minutes was asleep. Kate and Elliot went into the bathroom and he washed her up in the shower.

She dried herself and left him alone to clean himself up while she went to the bed to sleep beside her fiancé's best friend—her lover and their Master.

THE END

Also from Damien Dsoul...

THE TONGUE PATROL
SALES REP
Damien Dsoul

Lightning Source UK Ltd.
Milton Keynes UK
UKHW010631140621
385483UK00001B/177

9 781785 386374